HELLFIRE

THE DEADWOOD SISTERS: THE UNLUCKY
BOOK TWO

LISA MANIFOLD

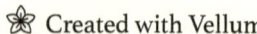

For my father
Who taught me to never give up.

CHAPTER ONE

hen a zombie comes shuffling through town in broad daylight, there aren't many options. I heard about it from someone in the shop. It was a day that all three of us—me, Deirdre, and Daniella—were working, and our customer, Kitty Knowlton, was in a chatty mood. She was a good source of gossip normally, but this had her all spun up.

"I heard on the scanner that they got a couple of reports of this fellow dragging along the highway. Down highway 85, the CanAm," she added. "I don't think the police have done anything, but the descriptions are just weird!" She gazed at me with wide eyes.

As the owners of Nightingale Tea & Herbs, my sisters and I were seen as people who might be able to explain about the weird and the strange. It was an unfortunate assumption, even as it was true.

The Nightingale women had been the protectors of

Deadwood since our Granny moved here in 1876, and while she and our mother, known as Meema, were gone, we kept up the family business.

And yes, we're all over one hundred years old. One hundred and seventeen, to be exact, but after a hundred, who's counting? Not me.

"That's crazy," I agreed with Kitty. "What do people say he looked like?" I kept my eyes on the tea I was measuring for her—a jasmine blend—because I didn't want her to see how interested I was.

"Well, everyone is saying his clothes are kind of ragged, and he looks gray," she finished. "How is it that gray is the main word?"

"I don't know. It is weird. Hopefully, they find him and get him some help. Sounds like he needs it," I added, handing over the tea.

Kitty paid and waved as she left.

I turned to Deirdre, who was hovering in the background. "Think it's a zombie?"

"What else is dragging along, raggedy, and gray? I mean, we could take some guesses."

Deirdre was good at the sarcasm.

"Who's up?"

Deirdre's finger shot up to the side of her nose. "Not it!" She shouted.

"Not it!" I heard from the back room where Daniella was stocking.

"Damn it, and damn the two of you," I sighed. I was never fast enough at our 'Not it' game. "All right. You're on the front. I need to go change my shoes." When dealing with zombies, it was better to have good boots. Zombies were not all that stable and physically, they tended to fall apart at any real provocation.

Literally.

"Just gross," I muttered as I walked through the back to find my boots. "Not how I saw today going."

"Maybe ask Zane if he's got anything going on?" Daniella suggested as I walked by her.

"Yeah, probably a good idea." I ignored anything else Daniella might have been suggesting.

Zane was our resident necromancer. Normally, we would have kicked his ass, and then kicked him out of Deadwood, but he'd showed up about a month ago and told me that John Henry Holliday, also known as Doc Holliday, yes, that Doc Holliday, also known as my grandfather, wanted to be free of us and he was there to help Doc get his wishes met and let Doc move on.

He also didn't do a lot in the zombie business, which was the necromancer stock in trade. He'd been helpful with our recent situation with... what would you call it? The Granny business? The pesky demon business? Our family history is screwed business? Regardless, he'd been really helpful since he showed up, so we'd allowed him to stay, with no ass kicking whatsoever. And he'd been helpful in the latest business of having to pick up stray zombies that were showing up in Deadwood.

There was also the small issue that I found I liked

him, but I wasn't dealing with that issue. And by not dealing with it, I meant that I was ignoring it every time my traitorous brain brought it up.

I tied on my hiking books and headed toward the back alley where we all parked. "I'm taking the truck," I yelled. Someone answered me, but I wasn't sure who it was. I grabbed a bag of chicken out of the fridge and walked out.

There was no way in hell I was taking my pristine 911 out to chase down some zombie. No way. We had an old truck used for the less... unsavory aspects of our calling.

As I climbed into the truck, I noticed that it kind of smelled like zombie. We collected grave dirt in this truck, which, as evidenced by its name, meant that there could be some of the dearly departed floating around in the cemetery compost. So the zombie smell, gross as it was, made sense.

"Call Zane," I told my earbuds. I loved these things. The phone dialed him.

He picked up on the second ring. "Desdemona," he said in his quiet, deep voice.

"You know anything about a wandering zombie?" I asked, speaking a little louder than normal over the rumble of the truck.

"No. It's not really my interest, as you know—"

"Yeah, yeah, I know. There wasn't accusation there," I cut him off. "Just wanted to know if you knew of any colleagues of yours in the area."

"No," he said slowly.

It was that slowness that caught my attention. "What?"

"Come and get me," he said and without waiting for an answer, hung up.

He'd been hanging around me too long. He wasn't this abrupt when we'd met. I obligingly turned toward the direction of Pearl Street, where our house was. Zane lived a few houses down from us.

Our house had started off life on Main Street, next to our shop, but Meema got tired of all the traffic, especially as Sturgis brought more and more people to Deadwood, and she'd badgered the town council until they let her move the house. We'd left the tea and herb shop where it was and moved home base up to Pearl Street. I liked where our place was now. It was quieter up here.

I passed by our house, which was quiet in the afternoon sun. I continued on to Zane's. He was waiting on the porch and came walking to me as I stopped in front of his place.

"What are you thinking?" I asked as he got into the seat beside me. He smelled good—like fresh air and honeysuckle. I thought it might be his hair gel. His hair was always just so.

"I don't know, but I've heard some rumblings. Not a lot—you know I'm not really considered a true necromancer," he added.

"No, I don't. You've never told me much outside of

your father trained you as a necromancer, and you moved away from it, and studied with a witch," I said, reminding myself that no matter how good he smelled, I'd known him a month, and didn't really know him.

He glanced at me. "I'll have to share that with you."

"Yes, you will. But at the moment, we need to see if the shuffler on the highway is really a zombie."

"Was your source good?" Zane asked.

I shrugged. "It was one of our customers. She's a police scanner junkie."

Zane laughed, a rich sound that filled the cab of the truck. "Don't you ladies have a scanner at home and at the shop?"

"Yes. But it's on low. Kitty is one of those people who has a cup of coffee and listens to it."

"Listen to you and your semantics," Zane said. "What did Kitty hear?"

"That a man in ragged clothes, who is mostly gray, is shuffling along the highway. She didn't say it, but I'd bet our Mr. Gray doesn't seem fussed by all the traffic, or anything most of us would consider a health hazard."

"How did he get there, if it is a zombie?" Zane asked.

"Good question," I said, taking a left onto Highway 85, also known as the CanAm. I wanted to head south, because Mt. Moriah Cemetery, where Granny and Meema were buried, was off of 85. It was a tourist destination, but not in regular use unless you had already purchased family plots. We still have four left, Granny being a planner. Mt. Moriah would be a good place to go if you wanted to dig up a body. Less chance of getting caught. We'd have to go and look after we checked out Mr. Gray-n-shuffling.

Zane and I were silent as we drove down the CanAm. When we got close to Deadwood Gulch, which despite the grand sounding name, was just the end of a gulch with nothing in it, I slowed.

"There. There he is." I pointed.

He *was* gray. I remember Kitty saying she thought it was odd that 'gray' was the main descriptor, but it fit. And he was raggedy as could be. I pulled the truck into the parking lot of one of the small motels and got out. I heard Zane's door slam, and we moved closer to the shuffling body.

"Oh, jeez," I said, putting my hand over my nose. I could smell him from here, and we were still a good twenty feet away. "If it's not a zombie, it's the worst non-bather I've ever encountered."

"Hello," Zane called.

The zombie stilled. Slowly, the head turned to look at us. Whoever this was, it wasn't one of our historical dead. I'd give it less than five years, given the clothes and general lack of decomposition.

"Eww," I said as bugs slid down his face. "Who were you, you poor thing? And what the hell are you doing out here in the daytime?" I always felt sorry for the zombies we caught. Even as I hated seeing them go after pets, they were still once people. And some asshole, probably a necromancer, or someone equally self-absorbed with their own greatness, had dragged this sad bastard out of the grave.

It was one of the reasons I liked to deal with zombies toot sweet. We never knew if it was someone who was related to those still here—we'd come across a couple of zombies over the years that we knew, and it was a shock—and I didn't want someone's mom to see their kid zombie-ing along one fine afternoon.

Another reason I hated those who created zombies. No respect for those still here. Like I said, self-absorbed assholes usually.

"Do you have any food?" Zane asked.

"Got it," I waved the bag I'd taken from the shop. As I opened it, I held out a piece of the chicken breast still in the bag and waved it in the direction of the zombie. "Hey, buddy? You hungry?"

The head turned even further to where Zane and I stood. I hoped it wouldn't fall off. That would be a lot of explanation we didn't need.

"Well, come on. We're happy to feed you if you come with us," I said. "Zane, go get the truck. We can't walk him along here." I pulled the keys from my pocket, tossing them to him without taking my eyes off the zombie.

The zombie slowly shifted, directing himself to me. I wondered why he was headed toward the gulch. There was nothing there, although it was surrounded by a couple of houses, a campground, and an inn on either side. I sighed. We'd need to look there, too. Since that appeared to be where this guy was heading.

The truck started behind me, and I walked backward, hoping no one passing by was looking too closely at our little tableau.

Zane stopped the truck behind me. When I glanced around, I saw that he'd backed it up. This was one of the reasons I liked him. It was obviously not his first rodeo in supernatural clean up. That made my life easier, fluttering heart aside.

I opened the tailgate and tossed the chicken breast inside. Then I backed away.

The zombie continued to shuffle forward, and when it bumped the tailgate, it stopped. Slowly, so slowly I wanted to scream, the head turned, the black eye sockets looking back to the gulch. It stayed very still, staring at the gulch for what seemed like a frickin' eternity.

Weird.

Then it looked forward to where the chicken breast glistened tantalizingly in the front of the bed of the truck, and it scrambled clumsily into the truck.

As soon as its feet, still in shoes, made it in, I slammed the bed of the truck, exhaling. "Let's get out of here," I said. I went to the passenger side and slid in. As I glanced over my shoulder to the bed, I could see Mr. Gray gnawing at the chicken.

"Where to? I haven't actually seen you in zombie removal action, despite the reputation," Zane said. He stopped the truck right before getting back onto the CanAm highway.

"We go to the shop first. We have a place where we can put him. We're going to need to see if he's from one of the cemeteries here. Then we put him back where he belongs," I said. I looked back again.

The zombie had stopped eating and was staring at Deadwood Gulch. As Zane pulled the truck out onto the CanAm, the zombie watched the gulch where he'd been heading. After the truck went around a corner, and Deadwood Gulch was no longer visible, he returned his attention to the chicken.

What was that about?

"Sounds like a plan," Zane said.

"Since you're still here, you helping?" I asked. I didn't want to ponder the zombie's odd behavior right this minute.

He nodded.

"I have extra gloves at the shop," I said. We needed to get back there now.

CHAPTER TWO

*W*e made it back to the shop in record time, and I directed Zane to drive down the alley and backed the truck into the garage that led to the shop. We'd gotten lucky with this building. It had a vault, as a former bank, and a basement to hold the vault, and a garage, presumably for the transfer of money in and out of the bank. It made it perfect for our uses. Granny had been smart when she bought this building.

"What are you going to do with him?" Zane got out, jerking a thumb at the zombie, who was still chewing on chicken breast.

"We have a place to keep him contained," I said. "We need to get him to the basement, though."

"You have more chicken?"

"We always have chicken. We waste a lot of it—or we did, until Beeval moved in."

Beeval was our house demon, who had recently helped me escape from Hell. In a major showdown with his former boss, Ashlar, also a demon and a major asshat, who had made a deal with my granny and screwed her over, and Sojin, Ashlar's boss, we had freed our family from the special attentions Ashlar was planning on visiting upon the Nightingales. Beeval had escaped Hell and come to live with me, and he was here for good.

Beeval was also a massive bacon fan. I could understand it, but it had gotten to the point where we had to buy a pig from one of the local farmers. Deirdre had brought home the not-quite-spoiled chicken for him one night and cooked it up. He loved it.

At least our bait meat wasn't going to waste. That was a good thing.

I pulled out another bag of chicken from the fridge, and opened it, walking back to the bed of the truck to wave it in the zombie's direction.

"He's got something pinned to him, Desdemona," Zane said, who had stayed close to the truck.

"What?" I kept waving the chicken. "Where?"

"Look at his front."

The zombie had been buried in a three-piece suit. Peeking out of his suit jacket, tucked near the pocket of the vest was a white scrap. Zane was right—it didn't belong. It looked like a piece of paper that had been pinned to the vest.

I couldn't see anything else because the zombie was moving towards me and my tantalizing chicken. I opened the tailgate and hoped he made it when he fell out of the truck. Otherwise, we'd have to dispatch him here, and this was harder to clean.

I backed away, and the zombie crawled forward, falling slowly out as his hands met air past the tailgate.

"This is really painful to watch," Zane said.

"Hence my major objection to zombies," I said, watching ours carefully.

With agonizing slowness, we coaxed the zombie downstairs. I got him locked in our cage—that always sounded so bad, even when I just thought the words—and Zane and I went back up to give my sisters the update. Zane went into the bathroom to wash his hands. I got it. I'd already washed the gross chicken off of me downstairs, but zombies had that effect. You felt like you wanted to scrub yourself all over.

A thought struck me, and I was smiling as I I came into the shop. "Hey," I said, walking into the public portion of the shop where Deirdre and Daniella were both working.

They both looked up. "Well?" Daniella said.

"It was exactly as we thought. He's a recent, like last five years." I sighed.

"Great. Cemeteries tonight?" Deirdre asked.

"For you two!" I laughed. "I have zombie detail."

It wasn't often I silenced my sisters, even for a

nanosecond, but they looked at me with twin expressions of 'WTF'? It made me grin even wider.

"Damn it," Deirdre said, looking back down at the tea in front of her.

"That 'Not it' game doesn't look so good, now, does it?" I asked, laughing.

They both shot me glares that could kill. I laughed harder. When I'd stopped, I said,

"I don't recognize him, but you guys need to look at him and see if you do, just in case he's local."

If he was local, and someone had seen him—we needed to be prepared for that.

Zane came back in, drying his hands on a towel. "What happens with him now?"

Any answer we might have given was halted by the ringing of the bell on the front door. A woman breezed in, followed by a man.

I recognized him. Wil Harwood, who'd saved my ass when I ended up in Mt. Rushmore in the middle of the night. It was right after I'd crawled out of Hell, and I'd been in rough shape. He was a ranger at Mt. Rushmore. He'd promised to look in on me, since he knew who we were. His wife was a regular customer.

They both had determined looks on their faces. I glanced at Daniella, to see if she remembered him. She nodded. Both of my sisters moved slightly away from the counter, and sort of pushed Zane along with them.

"Later," Deirdre said in a hushed tone. "Just go along."

Wil stepped forward even though his wife—what I presumed was his wife—had come in first. "Desdemona Nightingale, you look great."

"A lot more so than when we met," I said, smiling at him. "Is this Julie Ann?"

She nodded, obviously more reserved than her husband.

"Then I hope you're here to make your tea blend," I said. "I promised Wil it would be yours, and I've been waiting to hear from you."

"Did you call the police?" Wil wasn't going to let the business aspect of this visit slide away.

"I did. And I got hold of someone fairly high up the chain," I said, my smile widening as I thought of Ashlar's boss, or the Big Boss, as Beeval called him. "He got into a shit load of trouble for all that he did to me."

"Good," Wil said, his stern features relaxing.

I was touched. He'd been worried. I wondered why it had taken them a month to come in, but decided I was glad—it had been a rather crazy month for the Nightingales. Wil and Julie Ann showing up now was perfect timing.

The next hour was spent blending a perfect mix with Julie Ann, and then presenting her with a bag with a label that read 'Julie Ann's Afternoon Delight.' It made me feel good to do something that had nothing to do with our family curse, my ancestors, or the zombie in the basement. You had to take the good moments where you found them.

I walked them to the door, hugging first Julie Ann and then Wil. He let go, and then put his hand on my arm.

"If you ever need anything, let me know. I'm really glad to see you doing better. I've been worried about you, young lady."

"Thank you. And thank you for coming to check on me."

"I'm glad that Gerald Reid got what was coming to him," Wil added.

It took me a moment to remember that was the name I'd given Wil. I needed to start writing all these little details down. "Me, too, Wil. He was a complete douche—I mean," I stopped, remembering I was talking to my supposed elders. "Sorry. That slipped. He deserved everything he got." My satisfaction wasn't feigned.

"You're positively gleeful," Wil said. "That tells me he really got it handed to him."

"Oh, he did," I nodded.

"Thank you again for the tea," Julie Ann said.

I liked her. "You are welcome. Come and see us when you run out. It'll be on the shelves by then."

Her cheeks pinked at the thought, and with a final wave, the couple left. I watched them, enjoying the way that Wil rested his hand on the small of his wife's back. It made me feel good to see them.

"Who was that?" Zane came up behind me.

"Come on, I'll tell you about it," I said. I couldn't

remember if I'd told him about my rescue. But it would help pass the time as we dealt with our zombie friend. I'd have to comb the obituaries. We'd put an end to him later tonight, if Deirdre and Daniella could find a grave for him. If not, we had a place where we took our anona-zombies.

One thing Granny had always taught us was that even as zombies were a pain in the ass, they'd once been people. And they'd been dragged from the grave and given a bastardized life by some sicko, and so if we couldn't find their graves, then we were to put them to rest. She'd only been around until we were ten, but even then, there were zombies to be dealt with.

Zane and I walked down to the basement as I explained, and I gathered the camera. I liked to take pictures to see if we could find matches.

Yeah, it was a lot of work for a shuffling dead person, but it's what we did. We protected Deadwood, even after the people of Deadwood were dead.

No exceptions.

"We have to get that note off him," I said, remembering the scrap of whatever we'd seen on his vest.

"Maybe after he's less... mobile?" Zane asked.

"Well, he might be kind of messy. Seriously, what kind of necromancer were you?" I looked at him. "Didn't you do any work with zombies?"

A look of naked disgust passed across Zane's face. "That was my dad more than me."

"Who was your dad, Zane?" I liked the thought that

he wasn't as ghoulish as every other necromancer I'd ever met.

"Just a narcissistic asshole, like most of the people in my career path," he said, surprising me with not only the swear but the vehemence of his response. "I got out as soon as I could."

A shiver of---something---passed over me. Zane had made mention of his past before, but always with cryptic comments like this.

I contemplated his statement as I took pictures of the zombie, wondering if it was time to just hold Zane down and beat the truth out of him. He was carrying something, and it bothered him, and he was keeping a secret.

None of which sat right with me.

Particularly as we'd just had our own pull back the curtain and tell the truth moment in the Nightingale house.

Then I decided that he could tell me when he wanted to. And if he was hiding something that hurt me, or my sisters—then I'd kick his ass and put his head on a pike.

Figuratively, of course.

"Well, we have pictures of him, and maybe we can match him. Come on, let's see what else we need to do. I want to get back to the house to talk with Granny and Doc."

Zane nodded, still lost in his own memories.

I really hoped I wouldn't need to put his head on a pike, figuratively or otherwise.

CHAPTER THREE

I drove back to Pearl Street with Zane, who was still all broody. I'd let him brood for a little longer with me, and then he'd need to do that on his own time. I sighed. It seemed like there was too much to do in the past month.

And I couldn't shake the worry that Ashlar, the demon who'd dragged me to Hell—the real Hell—and taken Meema from us forever---would return.

In spite of what his boss, Sojin, had said. Ashlar didn't seem too smart in the self-preservation department. He had a lot of pride and anger, and those were dangerous to survival. Although he'd made it so far—I shook my head. I could make myself insane with this, going around and around in a never-ending circle.

It didn't matter. He was gone, banished from bothering the Nightingales ever again. If he did, Beeval and I would call Sojin. But I'd do well not to underestimate

Ashlar. He'd managed to survive all this time. And if none of our preventative measures worked, we'd just have to kill Ashlar. Because we still had the angel sword —the only thing known in this world that could kill a demon. I was thrilled we didn't use it before. It was an ace in the hole as far as demons were concerned. But I was honest with myself that I really didn't want to have to ever use it.

Once we pulled into the garage and walked up the stairs to the kitchen, I realized I didn't like the silence.

DeAnna, Dee, and Deana, the decedents of my sister Deana, had stayed with us for another two weeks after we dealt with Ashlar. Deana had just left, because prior to the phone call from us regarding Meema's death that changed their lives forever, she'd been about to open a business. Her mom and grandmother both practically pushed her out the door and onto a plane after we'd kicked Ashlar's ass. She'd managed to hang on for the two weeks—but eventually, her mom and grandmother sent her home. I got it, although I missed her. It had been wonderful having them all here. Even now, the house rang with talk and laughter. Having Granny's ghost here helped, although as she told us the story of her history, that had quieted things a little.

At least DeAnna and Dee were still here for the foreseeable future.

I thought back to one of the times we were all together right before Deana had left. We'd all been eating, and our ghosts, Doc and Granny, also still here for the foreseeable future, were hovering around the kitchen.

It was while we were all avoiding Granny's pronouncement that all the Desdemona's must die.

"So why did you make the deal with Ashlar?" Dee asked.

I liked Dee. She was quiet, and as I suspected, the bridge that smoothed over the passions of her mom, DeAnna, and her daughter, Deana.

Granny looked to Doc, which I found interesting. In the two weeks since she'd been back with us, I hadn't seen any return of passion between them, only a good friendship. It was nice.

Because honestly, no one wanted to have feuding ghosts in the house. A wave of sadness washed over me. I wished Meema was here to see this.

"Yeah, I get the feeling you haven't told us everything," Deirdre said. "Since we've moved on past the crisis point, how about you spill?"

"I told you that my family had some of the healing arts?" Granny asked.

We all nodded.

"Well, it was a bit more than that. My grandmother, we called her Nonni, and my mother, were known as wise women. What they knew was herbs, and teas, much like you do now," she nodded at my sisters and I. "Nothing scary, or mystical, just a knowledge of natural healing. But wise women were important for something greater—a compassion for women. To me, after watching Mama and Nonni, that was their gift." She stopped, lost in thought. "It was hard for women. You all have seen the attitudes around women change, so you have an idea of what I'm speaking of. Wise women, other women—they were the best people to care for women. And yet doctors, who were always men—hated wise women. In small communities, like the ones we lived in, it was a quiet but fierce competition. We used herbs. Doctors and apothecaries—many used things that would hurt people." She shook her head. "Not all doctors were bad. But the last town we lived in—my mother was friendly with the town doctor. Which made both of them suspect. The rumor began they were having an affair, that Mama and Nonni were witches— and we had to flee. The doctor," her eyes narrowed, "stayed and allowed my mother to take the blame for their friendship, even though the doctor had been teaching me because my mother saved his behind more than once." She took a breath, the anger still visible on her face.

"We ran. The woods—and there were a lot of them then—were always our friend. We could live off the woods, and that's what we did. We made it, oh, probably ten miles out of town. That was a full day's walk with all of our belongings, and we felt that we would be safe. We weren't."

"Granny?" I said. The mood in the room had shifted. Part of it was coming from Granny. Ghosts can affect the general atmosphere where they are if they are experiencing strong emotions. Most don't have them anymore, realizing that things in life were not worth all the effort and drama.

But whatever she was remembering was bad. I could feel it. All the hair on the back of my neck and arms stood straight up. Magic swirled around like an invisible fog. I could see that Deirdre and Daniella felt it too.

"What is going on?" Deana asked. She rubbed her arms as if cold.

"We didn't go far enough," Granny said flatly. "Two days after we'd fled, and made ourselves a small shelter out of branches, we were awakened by a group of men with torches pulling us from our pallets. They were rough, grabbing all of us inappropriately." Her lips thinned, but she continued. "The long and short of it was it the men were the local lynch mob, and they'd come armed with drunken courage and rope. They got the ropes tied around our necks. They were debating which branch to toss the ropes over when Mama started speaking. It wasn't anything magical," she added, looking around at us, "Because we didn't know any magic. But it was a Latin receipt for an herbal tinc-ture, and Mama started reciting it, pointing a hand at each of the men in turn. Nonni and I picked up her chant, and the three of us recited that mixture at least three or four times, getting louder."

Granny's form drifted a little. She still hadn't gotten the hang of keeping herself in place.

"Granny, you don't have to do this," DeAnna said.

"Yes, she does," Deana and Deirdre said.

"You OK, Granny?" I asked.

"You'd think it gets easier once you're dead," Granny said with a small, humorless laugh. "It doesn't. But thank you, DeAnna. I understand why you say that, but I do need to do this. As I said, we kept repeating it. Those men had never heard Latin in their lives. They had no idea what we were saying," she said scornfully. "I guess Mama figured if we were going to hang as witches, she'd do her best to make them shit their pants in fear."

Whoa. I couldn't remember Granny ever cursing. Ever.

"They stood still, transfixed. The fear was like another person in that little clearing in the woods. Then one shouted, 'Good riddance to witches', and they dragged us toward a tree. I had my herb knife in my skirt pocket, and I was able to take it from the pocket beneath my overskirt. I kept it curled in my hand, clutching it so hard that it sliced my palm. The men tossed first Nonni's, and then Mama's rope over a tree, and hauled them up." Her shade closed its eyes. "I will never forget the sight of them in the night, dangling from a branch, their feet struggling to find purchase on a floor that wasn't there."

She stopped.

"The men watched in silence, and then whooped and hollered, and carried on as mobs do. But then

Mama saved me. Her hands had been scrabbling at the rope around her neck—and they weren't tied very well, I suppose due to the drunkenness of our murderers. She managed to pull it away from her neck, and rasped out, 'Daughter, avenge me! Avenge us!'" Granny laughed. "You never saw grown men run like that. I've never seen it before or since. They just dropped the ropes and ran. Mama and Nonni fell to the ground and Mama, never one to back down, shouted at them in Latin again as they scurried away like the cowards they were." She looked at all of us. "That's why I didn't tell your mother anything. As Desdemona Nightingale, I was someone entirely new. I was not connected in any way with the woman who had been hung up over a tree branch."

I gasped. "Granny, that is horrible! What did you guys do after that?"

"Well, we gathered our things and walked all through the night. And then we walked all through the next day, not going on the roads, and sticking to the woods. We walked for four days straight, and then we set up a lean to in the woods." Granny sighed, her form drifting over towards the window.

Dee said, "Granny, I am so sorry. I almost can't get my head around it."

Doc spoke for the first time. "Things were different then, girls. Women were held in great esteem, as long as they didn't stray too far outside of the lines."

"That's for damn sure," Granny said. "Well, it was all

too much for my Nonni. Between hanging and the long walk to get away from that little backwards town, she took ill. She died two days after we stopped walking. And then it was just me and my Mama. We lived in the woods for, say, a year?" She looked around at us. "I can't really tell, because we didn't have calendars then, but it seemed like a year. It could have been less," she shrugged her shoulders. "But then my Mama got ill, and I nursed her as best I could. A lot of the fight had gone out of Mama when those men tried to hang us, and she just sort of drifted away." Granny crossed her arms. "We were in Missouri then, and that's where the handsy preacher made an appearance, and then I got myself to Kansas, so that I could make a new life for myself in Deadwood. I figured with everything I'd heard about the gold rush, which I'd heard not only before we left that little backwater town, but as I traveled, no one would notice one sort of pretty, young girl."

"Well, Doc did," Daniella said.

"Yes, he certainly did," Granny said, sliding her eyes to glance at the ghost of Doc. "And as I've told you girls, I'm very grateful that he did. But now you know," she said her manner becoming more businesslike and less emotional. "Now you know why I didn't tell your mother much about my past, and why I lied and said that my mother had died of cholera, and I didn't know where my father was. I didn't want anyone to ever know that my mother, grandmother and I had all been hung as witches."

"I just can't even believe that was still happening in the nineteenth century," Deirdre said. "It doesn't seem real."

"I'll tell you, I was fairly surprised myself," Granny said dryly. "But after that, that's why I made sure that first I, and then your mother, all stayed on the good side of the ladies of this town. I would bet my bloomers that we were run out of that town because some woman had her eye on the doctor that my mother was friends with."

"Were your mom and that doctor involved?" I asked.

A frown came across Granny's face. "You know, for the longest time I would've said no. But after all that I've learned, I think she might have been falling in love with him."

"Why would you say that?" Asked Deana.

"Because there is a curse on the Desdemona's," Granny said.

I sighed and rolled my eyes. "I could've gone the rest of the night without bringing up the subject," I said. Nothing would ever dim the moment when Granny told us that everyone with my name must die. It had happened right after we'd defeated Ashlar, so it had taken a bit of the shine off our win.

"Ignoring something will make it go away," Granny said glaring at me. "Excellent plan."

"Well, you certainly tried," Deirdre said.

I smiled gratefully at my sister. She wasn't going to let Granny off the hook, and I appreciated it.

But Granny was a Nightingale, and she had the

same spirit and refusal to back down as the rest of us. "Yes, I did! And look where that got us! I think now, with that famous hindsight, it would've been better for me to be honest with your mother, so that she could be honest with you girls. And then, we might have broken this curse."

"What triggers the curse?" asked Dee.

Everyone leaned in, the anticipation in the room growing to almost its own being. With all of the cleanup from our defeating Ashlar, there had been plenty of time for Granny to scoot away from answering this question. I even wondered if she told us this whole sad story to divert our attention from the curse.

Granny sighed heavily. "The curse has nothing to do with my family, girls. I shared that so you could maybe see why I didn't tell my sad story. No, the curse is entirely my fault. Once I knew I was expecting, I started doubling my efforts to work as a wise woman so that I could save money for after the baby was born. I was treating a woman, or rather I was treating her daughter." She stopped, and I could tell that she was attempting to gather her thoughts, to say the words right.

I understood that. You wanted to make sure that you said it exactly right, because you knew what you were about to say was the verbal equivalent of a bomb. I took a deep breath, bracing myself for what was coming.

"A woman name Mariah Connors, a woman who lost her husband, she'd come to me one afternoon. Her daughter was very sick. Of course, I agreed to treat the little girl, because that's what I did. And I felt for Mariah, because she was all alone."

"Why do I feel this is not going to go well?" Deana asked the room in general.

To everyone's surprise, Granny laughed. "Do these things ever go well? Would my history even matter if things had gone well?" She laughed some more, relieving the tension in the room. "Her daughter, Rebecca, had pneumonia. She been sick for a few days before I saw her, so it was intense. The pneumonia had a grip on the child. I visited her each day. Then Mariah came to see me one night and I wasn't home. I'd agreed to spend time with Doc. I knew he was leaving, but I couldn't help myself." She smiled at Doc, but it wasn't anything other than fond memories making her smile.

Or at least, that's what I hoped it was. Eww. No one needed that mental image.

"I didn't get home until the early hours of the morning," Granny said. "And by that time, Rebecca had taken a very serious turn for the worse. I hadn't been home long when Mariah was banging on my door, and she was furious with me. I went with her, but there was nothing I could do for Rebecca at that point." Granny smile faded. "Rebecca lasted the night, but she didn't see the dawn of the next day."

"I don't see what any of this has to do with the curse," Deirdre said.

"I'm getting to that, if you keep your hair on," Granny snapped. "What I didn't know at the time, was that Mariah was a witch. Now why she couldn't heal her own daughter, I will never know. But she was a witch, because I've been living with the fallout from that ever sense."

"What do you mean?" I asked.

"The day after she buried her Rebecca, Mariah came to see me. She told me that she had come to me because she thought that I had skill she did not. And that's when she told me that she was a witch. I asked her, why didn't you save your daughter? She slapped me in the face." Granny's hand moved up to her face almost involuntarily I thought.

"Mariah said that was not of my business, that she had come to me in good faith, paid me as a good customer, and that I'd had failed her. And she knew why," Granny said. "She came closer to me then, her eyes narrowed, looking like she would breathe fire and burn me up. I have to tell you, girls, I wasn't afraid of much at that point, but she scared me. She pointed her finger at me, and told me that because of me and my foolish choices over love, I, and every other Desdemona, would never be happy. We would always lose the ones we loved. That death would be our only constant companion." Granny rolled her eyes and looked up at the ceiling. "I will say that I was not kind at that point, girls. I told her that if she was a witch, she should have been able to help her daughter. And that she didn't get to come around here and be hateful to me, and that I wanted her to leave."

"She looked at me then, and I could see the empty depth in her eyes. All she said was, You will regret your hubris. He will never stay with you. And then she dropped her arm, and she walked out my door. I never saw her again," Granny said. "I assume she left Deadwood that night. After a while, I started to wonder if she even existed. If it was just a figment of my imagination, or some pregnancy fever my brain had dreamed up. And then I forgot about it," Granny said shrugging her shoulders. "Doc left, and I knew for certain that I was pregnant. That completely absorbed me. For years, I didn't even think of Mariah, although I always felt sad for the children I lost."

"What does this have to do with the curse, Granny?" Daniella asked, her impatience showing.

"Well, I lost Doc. But I chalk that up to he was going to leave anyway and put no stock in Mariah's words. That all changed when your mother fell in love." Granny sighed.

Daniella interrupted. "I'm going to assume that Burnsie wasn't the true love?"

Burnsie was the man I'd remembered Meema being married to. He disappeared before Granny died, although I remember it being around the same time.

"No," Granny shook her head. "He was not, although he was a good man. Don't ever doubt that, girls," she nodded at all of us. "He loved you dearly."

"That's good to know," I said, warmth flooding over me at the man who we'd grown up thinking of as our father.

Granny nodded. "So there you have it. Mariah Connors cursed me, and when Meema had you girls—"

"Yeah, how did you manage that, Granny?" Deirdre asked. "A multiple birth? During a time when twins killed women?"

Granny shrugged. "I merely helped your mother. I didn't have anything to do with it. I made sure all five of you had a fighting chance. With the medicine of the time, if it weren't for me, your mother would have died, and at least two of you with her."

"But how?" Daniella asked.

"I don't remember," Granny waved a hand. "It's been a long time."

"No shit," Deirdre said.

"No need for that," Granny snapped.

"So what's the curse?" Daniella asked. "How did you know it was real?"

"When you four were born, and your mother nearly died. I started to wonder if it was the women named Desdemona. But when Jack Fitzgerald died, I started to wonder. He died in a mining accident. He was the only one. No one else had any problems in the mine that day. Only Jack. And that's how I knew. I'd lost John. Your mother lost Jack. If you look back, my mother lost the doctor. Not that he was worth it," she sniffed, clearly not forgiving the man for having no spine.

Jack Fitzgerald. We'd read that name in Granny's diaries. I remembered that as she said his name. This must have been our father.

Understandable about the doctor Granny had mentioned in the story about how she and her mom and grandmother had to run. He sounded like a big candy ass. "Yes, but the curse wasn't in place then," I said.

"Do curses ever run straight and simple?" Granny asked, her expression bleak.

"How do we break it?" I asked. "And is it the Desdemonas, or the people they love?"

"I'm not sure," Granny replied. "About any of it. I puzzled over it for years, and I can't be sure."

"What?" Deirdre burst out. "You're not sure? There's still a Desdemona here!"

"Two," Dee said.

"What?" I turned to her.

"Mom was a Desdemona until she changed her name."

"Mom insisted on it," DeAnna said. "She told me it was time to choose a name for myself."

"Did you lose someone you loved?" Granny asked.

DeAnna looked away, her eyes distant, and her face more somber than I'd ever seen her. "I did."

"Dad?" Dee asked.

DeAnna nodded. "It was before you were born. He never got to meet you," she looked down.

Dee patted her hand.

Something inside me gave a tingle. Like the magical spidey sense. I had no idea why it would happen during this conversation, but I made a note of it.

"Then there's another," Doc said.

"Is it just the Desdemonas?" Deana asked.

"As far as I know," Granny said.

"What about you, Mom?" Deana asked Dee.

Dee and DeAnna exchanged a glance.

That was interesting. Seemed the Nightingale branch wasn't the only one with its secrets.

"I didn't lose my love. Your dad wasn't a..." Dee stopped, and it was obvious she was searching for the words, "A permanent fixture in my life."

There was an awkward silence, and then Deana hooted with laughter. "I was a mistake by the lake?"

"Never," Dee said, her relief palpable. She'd obviously never told this to Deana before. "He might have not been the best choice, but you're the best thing ever," Dee continued.

"Well, that's a relief," Deana said, rolling her eyes.

I could see the relief on Dee's face as well. She hadn't told Deana any of this because she wasn't sure how she'd be received. And here, with all our weird ass family, she'd spilled her beans, and it was fine.

At least, I hoped it was fine. I watched Deana for a moment. She hugged her mom, and I couldn't sense that she was putting on an act.

"Well, that was quite the bedtime story," Daniella

said. "How about we leave it there, and add it to the list of things to be sorted out?"

"What, because our list isn't long enough?" I laughed.

We all went to bed, and while the curse of the hedge witch, along with exactly what the curse meant, had gone on to our To Do list, we hadn't made any progress on it.

Mostly because the damn zombies kept popping up. They were like weeds. Poke weeds, or nettles. Stinging and annoying. The one today was the fourth one in two weeks. We'd already put three to rest, letting them finally die.

Our not being able to move on to the hedge witch issue was due in large part to us not being able to figure out who was creating the zombies and setting them loose to shamble away. Besides, the hedge witch curse had been around for a century. It wasn't going anywhere. Zombies were a bit more immediate.

Shortly after that enlightening conversation with Granny, Deana had left, although I knew she didn't want to. But her mom and grandmother were right. She needed to go.

There was nothing here but a never-ending curse and a plague of damn zombies.

I was going to twist the necromancer asshole in a knot when we finally found him. Or her. But it was probably a him.

They usually were.

$\mathcal{T}$he day after Zane and I found the zombie, I slept late. When I went downstairs, I found everyone talking. Granny and Doc were there.

I'd thought Doc wanted to leave, but it didn't appear to be that way. He'd told me he'd let me know when he was ready, and he hadn't said anything about it since. That made me happy. I liked having him here now that we weren't at war with him.

Everyone was focused on Granny. I listened while I got a cup of tea.

"That's all well and good, Granny," Daniella said. "But how do we stop it?"

They were talking about the curse again. Hadn't we covered this already? The curse was a big, fat question mark.

"I don't know," Granny said. "I wish I did."

"What did you tell my mother?" DeAnna asked.

"What do you mean?" Granny asked. It seemed as though she was stalling.

"I mean, did you tell her everything that you told us? Is this why she left Deadwood?" DeAnna responded.

The entire room got quiet.

Granny nodded slowly. "I did. I was so worried. Burnsie, your stepfather, had just left, and I was starting to believe that the curse took our loved ones. I was worried about you girls, and Meema. I didn't meant to, but I blurted it all out to her. She was so angry—it makes sense to me that this was why she left. The last thing she yelled at me was that now she couldn't be with her sisters. Then she told me to go to Hell, and slammed out of the room."

I looked at Deirdre and Daniella. Unexpectedly, tears filled my eyes. I could tell that they were remembering the night Deana left. We'd caught her sneaking out a window. She'd looked like she wanted to cry. I remembered trying to be calm, and allow her to have free will. But also remembered that I'd wondered, after she left, if I'd asked her to stay with us, rather than wishing her well, if she would have.

Deirdre grabbed my hand and gave me a squeeze.

"I'm sorry she left, but if she hadn't, we wouldn't be here," Dee said.

"That's true," I said, smiling at all Dee and DeAnna. "You wouldn't. And we miss Deana. We always will. But I'm glad you're here."

"I hate to break up such lovely family tranquility, but we still need to figure out how to solve this," Doc said, an edge of impatience breaking into his voice.

"Doc," Granny said. There was warning in her voice.

"No, Desi, I will not be silent! There has been too much silence in this house, too much of not asking questions and insisting on answers. We have lost Little Desi," he stopped, and looked down. But he continued, "I don't want to see another one of the girls meet a bad end. It's sheer luck that Desdemona returned. We cannot count on that luck."

I nodded. Thank Goddess Doc had moved us all back onto the right track. No one needed to be sobbing in their teacups. We had too much to do.

The phone rang, breaking some of the tension. Dee hustled over to get it. "Deana! I'm glad to hear from you." She listened for a moment, and then turned to me. "I think this needs you, Desdemona," Dee said.

After talking with Deana, I reluctantly gave her the name of a vampire I knew in Los Angeles. Zachary was a decent sort, for a vampire. He'd help her, or I'd take it out on him. He knew me well enough to know it. You never knew what was what with vampires. They had their own code. I found them full of pride and ego— generally a pain when it came to getting things done. But Zachary was all right. I liked him, vampire thing aside.

A few moments later, I got a text. It was from Zachary.

Did you send your niece to me?

I did. Give her the help she needs. I texted back. He would understand the inherent threat, which was what I wanted.

You owe me.

Done. I had no problem offering a favor to help Deana. You needed all the advantages you could get with vampires. They were crafty as hell.

That was the only good news—and that was a debatable piece of good news, because no one would deal with the vampires if they didn't have to—we had over the next few days.

We were making no progress on the hedge witch Mariah. It was as though when her daughter died, she disappeared from existence. Deirdre combed the message boards—there wasn't anyone who knew of Mariah. And Deirdre was careful in how she asked. If Mariah was around, she didn't need to know that the Nightingales were looking for her. Surest way to lose her forever.

Meanwhile, the zombies continued to show up. Zane and I were often the ones who went and got them.

"You know, we really need to find the source of them," I said to Zane after we stowed another one in the basement of the shop. "It's like a full house in there. A few more, and we're not going to have any more room at the inn. Who could be doing this? They're not getting anything out of it." I kicked at a rock outside the back of the shop. "Why are they continuing to make the zombies? Also, where are they getting them?"

We'd been doing checks of all the cemeteries. Nothing. Nada. Whoever it was had his or her own stash of dead folks because they weren't lifting ours.

Zane didn't answer right away. When I looked over at him, he was gazing thoughtfully at the brick wall. I'd learned, over the past month or so that I'd known him, that when he stared off into the distance, he was sorting things out. Even though it killed me, I kept quiet and let him sort.

Finally, he said, "Maybe that's the problem."

"What is?" I asked.

"We keep rounding up the zombies. Maybe we need to let them shuffle around for a bit, see where they're going. They all bang themselves on the bars once we get them in there," he nodded at the shop.

"Yeah, and usually end up offing themselves," I said, wincing. We'd just finished cleaning up one who had tried to wiggle through the bars of the cage. Gross didn't even begin to cover it.

"So the next one we hear about, we need to let it go." He was calm as he spoke.

I felt anything but calm. I threw up my hands. "Zane! That's not the answer!"

He gave me a mild look, not at all bothered by my response. "Why not?"

"We cannot have zombies traipsing through Deadwood! They bite, remember? Cats, dogs, babies, whatever's in the way. And no, the good people of Deadwood don't need to know that zombies actually exist! It's a miracle that we've gotten all of them out of sight before someone got a good look at them." I shook my head.

"Can't we spell them? I mean, can't you?"

"To do what?"

"So that regular people don't see them as zombies? Maybe they see them as homeless people, or hitchhikers, or something like that."

I opened my mouth to object and then closed it. It wasn't the worst idea in the world. "I bet we could do it."

"Now we just have to sell it at Pearl Street," Zane said with a grin.

Over dinner that night, after everyone had returned from the shop, and Zane and I had done another round of checking the graveyards, I brought the subject up.

The reactions were as expected. As I'd initially reacted, in all fairness.

"Wait," I held up a hand. "I'd like to take credit for this, but this line of thinking was Zane's."

Deirdre made a scoffing noise. "Well, necromancers have different ideas about zombies, don't they?"

Before I could cut her off, Zane answered.

"Well, yes. We don't see them like the rest of the magical community does."

"Yes, because necromancers see them as free labor, right?" Dee asked.

"Most do, yes. My point was," Zane said, "That necromancers aren't bothered by zombies like the rest of the world. So they would see nothing wrong with using a zombie to accomplish something. We keep spotting them, and picking them up. Maybe that's where we're going wrong. I think if we let one get through, we might have a better idea of who is creating them."

There was silence after he spoke. In our house, that meant people were mulling it over.

Or thinking of a cutting response. But since Zane wasn't a Nightingale, he didn't have that finely tuned sense of argument. Even the Deanas had it.

"How would we keep it from being seen by everyone else?" DeAnna asked.

"We'd charm it, or cast a spell over it," Daniella said. "We could spell the entire town, but that's a lot of work."

"Nobody needs that kind of work," Deirdre rolled her eyes. "Not with managing the shop, keeping up with the lessons, feeding the zombies we do have, and making unnecessary trips to the graveyard." She glared at me as she spoke.

"Hey," I held up my hands. "The one time we don't check is the one time the necro will pull from one of our graveyards."

"And the whole need to find a century old hedge witch," DeAnna continued as though I hadn't spoken. "I agree that we really don't need more work."

"Okay, so we spell the zombie," Dee said. "How?"

"Granny," Dee yelled.

I wondered if I needed to be concerned at how

comfortable the Ds were getting here at Pearl Street. We were going to ruin them for anything else.

"And there's something up with Deana," Dee said.

"Did she call?" Doc asked.

Dee shook her head. "I can just tell. Something's up. She will call, and it won't be good."

"Are you a seer?" Daniella asked.

"I don't know," Dee smiled, but it was a tired smile. "I'm a mother. Whatever it is, she's going to need us."

"All right, let's add that to the list," Deirdre threw up her hands.

"Zane, you studied with a witch, didn't you say that?" I asked.

He nodded.

"Can you help me, then? That way, it doesn't add to anyone else's to do list. We're usually on zombie clean up anyway."

"I might need to practice. It's been a while," Zane said.

Once more, I wondered what it was that had brought him here. Not that I was upset he was here –if anything, I was probably too damn happy about it.

We split up after lunch, everyone needing a break. Zane and I agreed to meet later to decide what spell we'd use, and give him a chance to practice.

As he walked down the street back to his place, I watched him go, my arms crossed. I felt, rather than saw, my sisters join me, one on either side.

"So," Daniella said, leaning into me, "What's up with the necro?"

"Nothing," I pulled my arms closer.

"Liar," Deirdre said.

"You like him," Daniella said.

"Which is good. One of us should finally get some action," Deirdre said.

"One, I don't know that I want action—"

Daniella snorted in disbelief.

"And two, I'm the one most likely to die, or have the person I care about die, remember? I'm the worst one to find any sort of romance," I said, a glum feeling creeping over me.

"It doesn't have to be," Deirdre said. That surprised me, as Deirdre often took what she called the realistic point of view of things.

"Well, none of us seem to have much luck. It's not just us, either. None of the D's kept a relationship. We're doomed to each other," I finished.

"That's not such a bad thing," Daniella put her arm around my waist, and leaned her head on my shoulder.

"Most of the time," Deirdre said. "Come on. Mooning over some hot necro guy isn't going to get anything done."

"Oh, shut up," I said. I turned and we went down into our basement. We kept our herbal counter there, and it was where we mixed up our spells. It was also where we held lessons for Dee and DeAnna.

As I tried not to think about Zane, I realized that

Deirdre was right. It didn't have to be this way. We'd gotten rid of one curse. We could get rid of another one.

After all, Mariah Conners, although a witch, was also human.

How hard could it be?

CHAPTER FIVE

I should have known better.

Dee and DeAnna got to work on tracking down Mariah Connors, and so far, had turned up nothing. People were easily lost in the late 1800's. And so many people were moving around. Without knowing about her family, or what happened to her after her daughter Rebecca died, we were literally seeking out a needle in a haystack. It was frustrating. I was glad that Dee and DeAnna had taken on that task.

Although I wasn't as busy as I hoped. The next two days brought no new zombies. I guessed that was a good thing. My sisters and I worked with Zane to perfect a warding spell for a zombie. If our theory was incorrect, and the zombies weren't headed somewhere in particular, it wouldn't be good for normal folks to see him.

I went to the shop and straight to the basement. Our

smelly friends were still bumping around in the cage. I noted, after watching them a for a time over the past couple of days, that they were all trying to go in the direction where we'd found the lone shuffler in the middle of the day. So I argued for keeping them alive a little longer. I wanted to see what happened when we let one loose. But I was tired of waiting, and I made a decision. The spell was as good as it was going to get. After all, it wasn't like we were new to this business of spells. I called Zane.

"Hey, let's spell a zombie, and see where he goes," I said. All of our current basement dwellers were male.

"All right. You at the shop?" he asked.

"Yes."

"Be right there."

Within fifteen minutes, he walked down the stairs, Deirdre and Daniella with him.

"We finally going to put this plan into motion?" Daniella asked.

I nodded.

"Which one is the freshest?" Deirdre asked.

The one that Zane and I had found near Deadwood Gulch was the slowest. He'd been slowing down more each day. He also still had the damn note pinned to him, and I was getting worried. Eventually, something gross would happen, and we wouldn't be able to read it when we finally got hold of it. Maybe now we could grab it.

All the zombies here, and Granny and all her issues

cluttering the house—my desire for order and tidiness was being tested. Everything around me was in chaos and disorder.

"Who did we catch last?" I asked Zane.

He studied all our zombies, and then pointed to one who was leaning against the bars. "That one."

"All righty, that one it is," Deirdre said. "We're going to need a lot of chicken." She went back upstairs and came down with an armful of bags.

"We need to get the lively one to the door," Daniella said, walking around the cage. "Without letting anyone else out."

"That's the kicker, right?" I asked, looking over the cage. Besides the one we wanted to get loose, there were four other zombies. Our first guy wouldn't be a problem. He was, as previously mentioned, moving really slowly.

"A broomstick," I said.

"What, you're going to try to teach him to fly?" Daniella asked.

We all burst into laughter.

"No," I got out finally. "We can use a broomstick, probably two, to hold off the other four so we can stop them. They're all moving more slowly—have you noticed that?" I asked.

Deirdre nodded. "Like their batteries are running down or something."

"Whatever it is," I said, "We can use that to make it easier to separate the one."

I grabbed one broomstick, and Daniella went upstairs to get the one out of the shop.

"Lock the door!" I yelled up to her. Our customers were used to us putting an 'Out to Lunch' sign in the door occasionally.

After a few moments, she came back down into the basement.

"Can you two handle this?" I asked Deirdre and Zane. "Zane, you hold the bait, so Deirdre can stop him if we need to."

"I could just tackle him," Zane said.

"Ew," Deirdre, Daniella, and I said together.

"No," I said. "Let Deirdre hit him with magic if she needs to."

"What are we going to do with him once he's out?" Daniella asked.

"Put the spell on him and let him go."

"Someone needs to follow him," Zane said.

"I will," I said. "Let's get him out, first."

Daniella and I moved to the sides of the cage, and carefully slid the broomsticks in. They overlapped about six inches in the middle of the cage. Hopefully, the zombies wouldn't be all revved up when they smelled chicken. Hopefully, their batteries were run down. Otherwise, we'd have a hard time holding them back.

Zane and Deirdre went to the side with the door.

"Ready?" asked Zane.

"Ready," everyone else said.

He opened the door, and waved the chicken breast inside the cage. All five zombies looked up, although some were slower. The one we wanted moved toward the chicken, and two of the other four did as well. The two of them bumped into our broomsticks and pushed against them.

"Hit them with a stasis spell, Des," Daniella said. "But not too hard."

"What? Oh, right," I said. I braced the broomstick under my arm, getting one hand up. I wiggled my fingers carefully, and the two zombies that were pushing against the broomsticks stilled. I stopped, not wanting to blow them to bits.

"Wave it more in his face, Zane," I heard Deirdre say.

The zombie we wanted out had stopped. The whole basement got quiet, and then there was a shuffle as the zombie started moving again. It made it out of the cage, and reached for the chicken Zane held.

Just as the zombie reached out, Deirdre hit him with a stasis spell, and he stopped, arms outstretched. Daniella and I pulled the broomsticks out of the cage as Zane shut the door behind the now free zombie.

"That was smooth," Zane said.

"Shut up," Deirdre said. "Don't jinx us."

"You're kidding, right?" Zane asked, looking to the three of us.

"Nope," Daniella said. "Sure way to send things into a pickle is to talk about how well they're going."

Zane snickered, but didn't say anything more.

"All right, let's get the cloaking spell on him," Deirdre said.

Together, the three of us cast the spell.

"How do we know if it works?" Zane asked.

"Well, let's feed him, and see what happens."

"We're just going to let him loose?" Zane's eyebrows were high.

"Wasn't that your idea?" I asked.

"I guess it was," Zane said.

"Little different when you have to put the ideas into practice, isn't it?" Deirdre asked, a grin on her face. "Don't worry, necro boy. You and Desi get Shuffles here out the back door, and Daniella and I will go out front and make sure he isn't harassing the populace." She and Daniella went up the stairs.

The zombie, released from the stasis spell, reached for the chicken Zane still held. Zane jumped, and let the chicken go.

"We should feed the rest," I said, lifting the stasis spell off the four left in the cage. I tossed chicken from two more bags into the cage, and for a time, the only sound was the chewing of the zombies.

Which was all sorts of gross. That's all I'll say.

"You think this will work?" Zane asked.

"You're having doubts?" I asked.

He shrugged. "I don't know. More like seeing all the things that could wrong."

"Welcome to our world," I said cheerfully. I hadn't

operated in the realm of better than fifty-fifty odds in years.

The freed zombie finished the chicken and took a few steps toward us.

"Wake up," I said, poking at Zane. "Let's get him out of here."

We held chicken out of in front of us, luring the zombie along through the garage. "Hold him there for a sec," I said. I darted outside to look around. There was no one in the alley, thank Goddess. Running back in, I opened the garage door wider, and let the zombie out. We tossed the chicken out away from the building, and went back inside, shutting the garage door behind us. Then we both stood at the back door, watching to see what the zombie did.

For the longest minutes ever, it stood there, chewing. How the hell were they so hungry? They didn't have any sort of digestion. It baffled me.

"Where does all the food go?" I whispered to Zane.

He shrugged. "I was always taught it gave them energy to keep going. I didn't inquire."

"Like, are there zombie bathrooms?"

Both of us started laughing, trying to be quiet, but not succeeding. We leaned against the door, laughing.

Thankfully, the zombie paid us no mind. It—he— finished the chicken, and then the head swiveled back and forth.

"Oh, shit," I said.

"What?" Zane asked. His cheeks were pink from our laughing.

"If he's headed down where we've been finding these guys, it's going to take all day to follow him.'"

"I didn't think about that," Zane looked out the window at the zombie, who'd shuffled past the door, heading out toward Shine Street. We were in the corner building on Main and Shine Streets, and he was on track to run right into tourists in a few minutes.

"It might stop our experiment before it ever gets started if the zombie comes off like a drunken weirdo." I opened the door. "Hey!"

The zombie kept going.

"We have to get him, and bring him down the CanAm," I said, looking at Zane. "Go tell Deirdre and Daniella where we're going, and I'll get the truck. Meet me on the corner."

He nodded and went toward the front of the shop.

I ran to the truck, got it going and followed the zombie out to Shine, and then Main Street.

"Shit," I swore. Why didn't we think of this before? I'd forgotten how far away we'd been finding the zombies. They didn't need to shuffle through a couple of miles of tourists and the general public.

As I pulled out onto Shine Street, Zane came around the corner. Deirdre and Daniella were with him. They came to my door. "Now you want to toss him in the truck?" Daniella's nose was wrinkled, no doubt with disgust.

"Yes. It's nearly two miles down the CanAm," I said.

"That's if that's where they're going," Deirdre said.

"It's where he's going," I said. "Quick! Get him in the back!" The zombie had come around the corner, and was walking down Shine.

"Oh, crap," Daniella whispered.

Two ladies were walking up Shine, and the zombie was going to have to go right past them. We couldn't grab him and just toss him in the truck if he looked like anyone else—I was betting I wasn't the only one who was holding my breath as the women walked by the zombie.

One said something to him, and he didn't respond.

She glared, saying something to her companion. They both gave him the stink eye, but kept going.

"He can't look like himself," Daniella said. "It would have been worse than stink eye."

"My thoughts, exactly," I said, leaning out of the window to look behind me.

A car came up behind us, honking.

"Go around!" Deirdre shouted. They drove around, the woman in the passenger seat glaring, and the man saying something that I couldn't hear.

"Get this guy in the back," I muttered. "We're already attracting too much attention."

"You have chicken?" Daniella asked.

I handed her the bag I'd brought with me. That's Rule Number One with zombies—never go anywhere without food for them. You never know when you're going to need it.

"Let's see if we can move him along," Zane said. He walked across the street to where the zombie had stopped.

Yeah, at this pace, if we left him to his own devices, he'd never make it there. At least not in this century.

As I watched in the rear view mirror, Zane put his arm along the zombie's back, and pushed. The zombie stumbled, but didn't fall.

A car turned onto Shine, braking to a halt because Zane and the zombie were in the middle of the road.

"What's the problem?" a man yelled out the window.

"Too much to drink," Zane called back, shaking his head. "Sorry, man."

The man in the car pulled his head back in, waving and smiling.

It was weird how much you could pass off as drunkeness.

As the two of them got close to the truck, Deirdre and Daniella walked to the back and opened the tailgate. Daniella threw a chicken breast in the back.

The zombie hesitated, and then crawled in. It was the slowest, most painful thing I'd been involved in in ages.

Deirdre slammed the tailgate shut as Daniella came back to my window. "Get out of here," she said. "Too many people have seen us already."

"You all coming?"

She shook her head. "Take Zane. We need to be in the shop so it looks like any other day. We'll just tell people you have drunken louts for friends."

"Great," I said.

Zane got in the passenger side, and we took off.

"Keep an eye on him," I said.

Zane watched the zombie as I turned onto the CanAm.

"Where do you want to let him off?" he asked.

"A little further down." I didn't want to be too close to the trailhead that was right off the highway. We had a popular trail that ran between here and a couple of towns south along an old railroad track. No need to scare the hikers.

When we were a short distance from the hotel parking lot where Zane and I had grabbed the zombie last week, I pulled off the road along a large section of shoulder. "Let's let him go here."

I remembered thinking the one zombie we'd picked up was really interested in Deadwood Gulch, and I wanted to see if this one was as well. All our caged zombies bumped along one side of the cage, facing the same direction, with no regard for chicken or us. It was the same direction as Deadwood Gulch from the shop —and I might be completely off the mark, but I wanted to see.

Zane got out, grabbing the bait bag, and opened up the tailgate. The zombie shuffled along the truck bed and then fell out. It picked itself up slowly, and walked to Zane. He circled into a u-turn, and led the zombie away from the truck. I rolled up my window as the zombie passed, and as soon as it made it beyond the truck, I got out.

"I feel like you're doing all the heavy lifting," I said.

"I feel like we dodged a bullet. Whose idea was it to let this guy just wander?"

"Some necromancer," I said, smiling.

"Yeah, not one of my better ideas."

"Well, perhaps not as well thought out as it could have been." I said.

"Coming from a Nightingale that means nothing."

"Ouch," I faked a wince.

"Well, you three are more the go in and kick ass and plan later."

"There's some planning. And if there was some lacking here, look at it as fitting into your environment," I said.

We grinned at one another, and I felt a zing run through me that had nothing to do with the magic that was always at the tips of my fingers. This was something else. I knew what it was—I just didn't want to face it.

"Desdemona," Zane began.

I looked around him. "Hey, there he goes. Get in," I turned and climbed back into the truck. A moment later, Zane followed.

Pulling out across traffic, I stopped further down the highway shoulder, pulling off ahead of the zombie so that we could watch him. I reached under the seat and grabbed a cloth bag.

"Come on," I said.

"What are we doing?" Zane asked.

"We're known around here for stopping and looking in the weeds at weird places. We've spent a lot of time cultivating that," I said, heading for the weeds along the side of the parking lot. "It lets us stop and get things done without looking suspicious."

"Clever," Zane said, bending down next to me.

"We've had some time to come up with these kinds of things," I said, keeping my head bent, but still watching the zombie.

Zane and I stayed where we were for what felt like eons, both of us watching the zombie, and not speaking.

Zane broke the silence. "Can I ask you something?"

"Sure," I said.

"Would you like to go to dinner with me?"

I blinked, and then looked at him. "What?" I asked, not sure what I heard.

"Dinner. You. Me. Together," he said. "Yes or no?"

A wave of long-forgotten emotions washed over me. I looked into his stormy green eyes, and I felt lost. Not in a bad way, though. In a scary good way. It made my skin tingle. And again, the tingle had nothing to do with magic.

I hadn't even gotten this tingle when Marcus Gibby had held my hand in my sophomore year of high school —my real sophomore year. I'd loved him since second grade, and to have him hold my hand had been one of the biggest thrills of my life. Even with all my boyfriends over the years, nothing had come close to the touch of Marcus Gibby's hand.

Until now. With Zane looking at me like he wanted to kiss me. I opened my mouth to respond when a screech of brakes broke the silence.

CHAPTER SIX

*W*e both turned to see the zombie drifting out into the road as cars swerved around him.

Zane muttered something, and marched out to the zombie. He was grumbling, but not anything that I could make out clearly.

"Don't let him bite you," I said loudly, so he could hear me over the traffic. "That will completely suck."

You don't turn zombie if they bite you. You do get sick as shit, and are exposed to all sorts of gross things. I mean, have you seen their teeth? Disgusting doesn't even begin to cover it. So while it's not going to turn into the apocalypse if one gets a hold of you—it's not pretty.

The zombie stumbled around a bit, then righted itself, and began heading south on the CanAm. Zane came back over to stand next to me, and we watched its progress, if you could call it that, in silence.

"Does it seem like it's losing steam?" Zane asked.

I narrowed my eyes. "It does. Kind of like that one we picked up here. That's the slowest one in the cage now." I'd never seen zombies get tired. That was just what this looked like—an exhausted zombie.

"So yes or no to dinner?" Zane asked. His arms were crossed, and he wasn't looking at me.

This was it. I should be paying attention to the zombie, to the fact we had yet another curse hanging over our heads, to all sorts of other things but instead —"Yes," I said, feeling happier than I'd felt in a long time.

"Good," Zane said. He didn't speak again.

"Look," I breathed.

The zombie had stopped, and it was right in front of the ravine that led to Deadwood Gulch.

"I was right," I said. "It was Deadwood Gulch." I turned to Zane. "We need to follow it."

"No, it's too close to dark," Zane objected.

"I'm not afraid of the dark," I said.

"Neither am I, but heading off into the dark and into a situation we don't know, facing who knows what— come on, Desdemona, we are smarter than that."

I watched the zombie stumbling into the brush. It would be in the trees in a few minutes, even at the slow pace it was moving. I sighed. "You're right. But damn, I just want to find out where it's going!"

"Is there anything back there?" Zane sounded completely normal again.

"Not for years and years," I said. "Nothing currently."

"Good place to hide, then," he said.

"Yes."

As we watched, the zombie made it through the trees. I sighed again. I hated letting anything get away.

"We'll find it," Zane patted my arm, his hand lingering for a moment. "Let's get back."

We walked back to the truck, and as we got in, Zane said, "What's your favorite meal?"

That was easy. "Crab Hollandaise burger at the Saloon No. 10."

He laughed. "That's where we met."

A smile that felt big and goofy spread over my face, and I couldn't stop it. "Yes, it was."

"Saloon No. 10 it is. How about tomorrow night?"

"All right," I said, feeling my heart beat faster.

"I'll pick you up."

"No," I said, looking over at him. "I'm not ready for questions. You know where I live, who I live with," I added. "I'll meet you there."

He didn't like my answer, but I knew he saw the sense in it. At least, I thought so.

"Seven, then?" Zane asked.

"Yes," I said, smiling again.

As we drove back into town, I asked, "You want to come back to the shop with me?"

"Sure."

We parked out back and went into the shop where Deirdre and Daniella were closing up.

"Where's our friend?" Daniella asked.

"Somewhere in Deadwood Gulch," I replied.

"Good call," Deirdre said to me.

"We need to go check it out tomorrow. The zombie went straight in, like a homing pigeon."

"Someone's got to mind the shop," Daniella said.

"Let's talk about this later. I'm ready to get home," Deirdre said.

"Hang on. I have to wash up," I said.

When I'd gotten as much of the chicken goo and what felt like zombie goo (even though I knew there was no such thing on me), off, we all left, Zane and I driving back to Pearl street in my 911.

"You want to come over for dinner?" I asked.

"No," Zane said, and he had a weird note in his voice.

Was he regretting asking me out? I looked over, and he was looking out the window. What the fuck? What had happened in the short time it took to drive back into town?

"All right. I'll drop you off."

He nodded, and when I got to his place and pulled in, he turned back to me. "I'll see you tomorrow night. I don't think I'll be around until then. I have some things to tackle tomorrow."

I looked at him for a moment. "Is everything all right?"

Zane leaned over, and covered my hand with his. "It is. I've just been putting off some things, and I want to get them out of the way."

I understood that, even as I didn't feel completely reassured. "OK. I'll see you tomorrow, then?"

He nodded, and flashed me his amazing grin, and then he was gone. I waited until he got in the house, and drove back to ours.

When I came into the kitchen, I was bombarded by nearly the entire family, ghosts and all.

"Where's Zane?" Doc asked.

"I dropped him off. He had things to do," I said, feeling defensive and trying really hard not to be defensive. Then they would all know that something was up, and I'd be screwed.

The phone rang.

Thank Goddess.

Deirdre was closest. "Hello, Deana. I'm glad you called. Your mom is going bananas, even though she's trying not to show it." A moment of silence and then, "Oh, shit. Should I put this on speaker?" Deirdre turned to us. "All right, hang on. I'm going to yell." She held the phone against her midsection. "Dee! Daniella! Get down here!"

There was a moment as everyone came into the kitchen, and Deirdre nodded, putting the phone up to her ear again. "Okay, I have everyone here. I'm putting you on speaker. What's going on, Deana?" She pressed the speaker button.

There was a sigh on the other end of the line. Deana sounded far older than her years. "I'm up a creek with a vampire."

All of us were silent, digesting what that might mean. I said, "How the hell did you end up the creek? Wasn't this just you going and talking to Zachary?"

Deana sighed again. "It's all complicated and basically, a shit show. Let me tell you, and then you can yell at me later, okay?"

"She's totally one of us," Daniella said in an undertone, which made all of us laugh a little.

Deana went through everything that had been going on.

"You were right," I whispered to Dee. She'd been worried about Deana for a couple of days now.

"I hate that I usually am," she whispered back.

"Well," Deirdre said. "You are up a creek."

"Good to know your assessment of the situation is accurate," Daniella said.

"Mom?" Deirdre said.

"I'm trying to calm myself, Deana," Dee answered.

"Couldn't you have said no?" DeAnna asked. "Kel was such a... such a shit!"

This had all began because Deana took a case to help an old friend named Kel. We'd need to find out who this Kel person was that had dragged Deana into a veritable snake pit of vampire bullshit. They were up there with the necromancers as pains in the asses, in addition to all the other things you had to go through to deal with them. And now my niece was neck deep in it. But that would need to wait. Right now, Deana needed solutions.

We talked for a while, going over the best strategies for Deana. Now that she was out as one of us, she had to be strong, take a stand. Otherwise, the rest of the supernatural world would run all over you, take all your shit, and leave you in the dirt. It was every man for himself out there. I was glad that we didn't have to go anywhere —that we had a home base here, in Deadwood, and that we'd been here before pretty much everyone else. So people knew to stay out of our turf. Well, until now, I thought, remembering I needed to share the news about the zombie heading into Deadwood Gulch.

Deana talked Dee and DeAnna out of going back to Los Angeles, which I was glad to hear. Even as I understood their desire—I also wanted to go in and kick Kel's ass for getting her into his mess. I got it. But if Dee and DeAnna went back, it would be adding targets to themselves that they didn't need. The target on Deana was bad enough. I nearly laughed out loud when she asked for vampire spray.

I brought the focus back to solving Deana's concerns. "Let's focus on the immediate problem. Vampire spray," I laughed at the idea. "I could sell a metric ton if we actually manage to make it. On the very down low, of course."

"I'm really glad I called you all," Deana said.

I could hear it in her voice.

"Why didn't you do it earlier?" Dee asked.

"Because I didn't want to worry you," Deana replied.

"I've been worried," Dee said. "I can tell when you're in trouble."

Deana sighed. "I know, Mom. I'm sorry."

"If there's one thing the last month has taught us, we're stronger together," Dee said.

"Isn't that what I've been saying?" DeAnna exclaimed. She rolled her eyes.

"I have some ideas," Deirdre said, getting to the business at hand. "If your ears are burning for the next couple of days, Deana, just know that your mom is complaining. But we'll let her vent at us."

"Thanks," Dee said dryly.

"How about two days? I have just under five days to figure this mess out," Deana replied.

"All right. You call us, Deana. If we don't hear from you in forty-eight hours, we're sending in the cavalry," I interjected. I didn't want to let Dee rip into Deana. Well, not right now. That was a mother's prerogative, but at the moment, it wouldn't help anything. Given my experience with Meema, it was better done in person than on the phone.

"Deane, please be careful," Dee said.

"I'm trying as hard as I can, Mom," Deana sounded like she was holding in frustration.

"That's what worries me, honey," Dee replied.

"Come on, lazy—oh, hey, Doc," I said.

Doc had drifted over, obviously listening to the call. "Darlin'?" he said toward the phone.

"Hey, Doc," Deana answered.

"Are you all right?" he asked.

"Not really. But I think I will be."

"You mean you finally took your head out of your backside and leaned on your family?"

"Wow. Shamed by the family ghost," Deana laughed a little.

"That's what we're here for, darlin'," Doc shot back. He looked over at me and winked. "To tell all you still locked in the mortal coil what you're doin' wrong."

"You're so good at it, too," I said. "Deana, keep the faith. This happens to us all the time. The way forward will show itself."

"I hate to say it, but listen to Miss Wise Guru," Deirdre added.

"Okay. I'm going to hang up now," Deana was still laughing. "Love you," she added.

"Love you," we all chorused.

Deirdre hung up, and there was a moment of silence.

"Whatever she's involved with, we don't even know the half of it," DeAnna said.

"Nope, we don't," Dee added in.

"Didn't she just tell us everything?" I asked, feeling a little confused. But I was thankful that the current Deana crisis meant no one was asking me about Zane.

Which, had I not been saved by the phone, would have occurred. Interrogation style.

"There's never full disclosure with Deana," Dee said. "She's so stubborn, so determined to do it on her own, not asking for help—"

We all started to laugh, and after a moment, even Dee joined in.

"Yes, I can see where she gets it," Dee said. "But can you really help her?"

"I think the idea of vampire spray is awesome. We seriously could make a mint," Daniella said.

I nodded. "I wasn't kidding. We'd just have to be super low key. And we could never let anyone know we made it for Deana."

"Then can we get started?" Dee asked. "The sooner we get this to her, the better I'll feel."

"Liar," DeAnna said, but she patted Dee's back affectionately. Dee leaned her head onto her mother's shoulder.

Moments like these made me miss Meema so badly it was a physical pain.

I inhaled deeply. "All right. Let's get started. I have to go into Deadwood Gulch tomorrow, so I'd like to get a start on this." I went toward the basement stairs.

"Hold up a moment," Doc said. "You want to tell us what happened tonight?"

I stopped, turning slowly. "With what?" I remembered that I hadn't told them about the zombie. OK—

"With what?" Doc had his hands on his hips as he

looked between my sisters. "With what, she asks. With Zane, the handsome necromancer from down the street?"

Heat raced up my neck and into my face. Damn it all to hell. Just what I didn't want to talk about. How the hell did they know *anything* had happened?

But no one spoke, obviously waiting on me to say something.

"Well?" DeAnna asked.

"We're having dinner tomorrow night," I said.

Everyone in the room whooped. Like, cowboy, rodeo style whooping.

My face got warmer.

Deirdre hugged me. "I'm so glad. It's about damn time!"

"What's that supposed to mean?" I glared at her.

"You've liked him since he walked in the door. I think he's liked you, too. We've all been wondering when one of you would finally get it together and do something about it. You have to be the slowest couple to happen on the planet."

"Really? Everyone?" I found that I was whispering, something I didn't care for.

Daniella came to stand next to us. "Yes, everyone. But you're so damn stubborn, and scare off people. I wasn't sure he'd get past all the Des defenses."

I started to laugh. "Is there a pool?"

For a moment, neither of my sisters said anything, then Daniella nodded.

"Who won?"

"I did!" Dee came over, laughing. "I said the shared zombie adventures would be the thing that did it."

"What? Why would you think that?" I asked. I wanted to be mad, but I couldn't.

"Because you're a Nightingale. And we like men for impractical reasons. Most of whom don't stay around. But I think Zane is different."

"How?" I threw up my hands. "I'm a Desdemona, remember? Either I die, or the one I love dies."

"We don't know that," Dee said.

"We know that something happens," I shot back. As I said it, I realized that this was part of the problem for me, in addition to my normal reticence to romance.

"We didn't know that until now," Deirdre said. "And this time, this could be with someone you don't have to hide from."

"Well, that's true," I said. "But I think you're getting ahead of yourselves." I wanted to put this discussion to bed. "It's just dinner."

Dee laughed. "Yes, honey, that's what we all say." She patted my shoulder and walked away.

I watched her, wondering why she made me feel like the younger of the two of us.

"It's not a bad thing, Des," Deirdre said. "All I'm saying is you should give him a chance."

"He's a good guy," Daniella said.

"I know that!" I snapped. "There's more to it than just being a nice guy!"

"There always is," Doc drifted over.

"You're not going to offer advice," I said, giving Doc the stink eye.

"I may not have been lucky myself, but that wasn't because I didn't recognize good women," Doc said.

"Just not enough to stay with them," Deirdre rolled her eyes.

As Doc opened up his mouth to retort, Deirdre held up her hands. "Peace, peace! I'm not trying to fight—"

"You sure she's a Nightingale?" Daniella said to me quietly.

"I heard that. Yes, I'm sure. I'm maturing," Deirdre said. "Too bad I'm the only one."

All three of us glared until Deirdre stuck out her tongue, and we all burst into more laughter. That was one of the best things about my family. We fought hard, held our positions, and didn't give up. But we were always ready to let things go to laughter.

You couldn't make it for a long life without it. We'd have killed one another years ago otherwise.

"Can we drop the subject of my barely there love life? If I promise to give you a postdate recap?" I asked the room at large. "And no harassing Zane, either!"

"Where is the fun in that?" Doc asked. He smiled. "Of course, Desdemona. We will be discreet."

The entire room started laughing, even me. "Since that's our strong point," I said, rolling my eyes. I was relieved that no one had any real objection, even if I wouldn't admit that to anyone else.

"All right, now that we've had our fun, let's get down to business. What's up with the zombies?" DeAnna asked.

"Has anyone gotten the note from that zombie that's been there a while?" I asked, thinking about the four we still had at the shop.

Daniella glared at me. "You couldn't just get the damn thing?"

So much for the peace and love.

I shook my head. "Every time I've tried, he's been snappy. Like it's the only time all day he gets lively now."

"Do you think it's important?" Dee asked.

Granny drifted in, looking a little lost. "Sorry, girls, I got caught upstairs."

"Granny, you need to get better at ghost," Daniella said. "Doc, can't you help her?"

Doc shook his head. "I have offered advice, Daniella. It's an individual thing for each spirit. We are not all the same."

Granny shrugged. "I'll get used to it. What did I miss?"

"I have a date, Dee won the betting pool, there's a note on one of the zombies that yes," I said to Dee, "I think might be important, but I don't know. And Zane and I—" I stopped to let the comments happen. They needed to get it out of their systems. "Zane and I let a zombie go and it went straight to Deadwood Gulch."

That stopped all the teasing.

"Shit, you were right," said Dee.

"You won the pool? Dang it," said Granny in an undertone to Dee. "I was way off. Good job, girlie," Granny nodded.

I ignored Granny. My love life, or whatever there was to it, was five minutes ago as far as discussion went. "Yes. I wanted to go in tonight, but Zane was concerned we'd be headed into the gulch as it was getting dark."

"That's sweet," DeAnna said, her face deadpan.

"Nope, nope, nope!" I said as I saw the others react to her words. "We're not going there. This is about us, and our job. We protect Deadwood. And that's what we're going to do. Tomorrow, we're going in to see who the hell it is thinks it's all right to come into our house and send zombies out willy nilly." I found that I was angry, and it had nothing to do with all the teasing. Whoever it was that was here had a shit ton of nerve.

My words stopped the laughter. Thank Goddess.

"You're right," Deirdre said. "So you saw the zombie go to the gulch? Like you thought," she added, giving me the credit of my earlier observations.

I appreciated it for what it was and nodded. "I remembered that zombie with the note was actually hesitating about following the chicken. It kept looking toward the gulch. Zane and I let this one today go down the CanAm, and it went straight to the gulch. Like it was going home." I left it be that I'd been trying to tell them this before my date became the topic of conversation.

Despite my embarrassment at being the subject of such conversation, I got it. Once we were told that not only were we witches, but that once we reached our twenties, we really weren't going to age—the whole romance gig became a thing of worry.

And no one wanted to bring any more kids into this. In that sense, I got why Deana had left, and stayed gone. Even if it was due to Granny that she left—if I left, and had a chance to be someone else, to have a child —would I?

I didn't want the choice. I loved my life. But it did mean that chances for love were limited, even without Mariah Connors and whatever the hell her curse was hanging over me and any other Desdemona.

"All right, what do we need?" Daniella said.

"I don't think we all need to go in there," I said. "I'll go and check it out. I'll be discreet," I added, seeing Deirdre roll her eyes. "Just looking. No magic, no anything. I want to get an idea of what we're up against. Because frankly, I'm tired of surprises."

"That's true," DeAnna said. "This is your—well, our, town," she stumbled a little, "And the rest of the magic world should respect that."

"It's not like there's not places without the Nightingales," Dee said.

My heart swelled. This, from DeAnna, the most reluctant of our family, warmed me in a way I hadn't expected. "Well, let's eat, and then go see about some anti-vampire spray."

Dee looked worried. "I should be concerned about my kid, and here I am all happy that I won the pool."

I hugged her. "Don't beat yourself up. We all have to laugh, or we'd go insane and knife each other. Deana would be laughing with you." That made her smile.

And we all split up to get a meal together.

Thankfully, my date was no longer the topic of discussion as we debated what might work to help Deana neutralize a vampire. The argument continued into the basement and our mixing table.

It was the best night I'd had in ages. Zane had some competition for tomorrow. I was smiling when I went to bed.

CHAPTER SEVEN

The next morning, I got up and the feeling of teamwork was still strong here on Pearl Street. We got breakfast together, fed Beeval, which was a job within itself, and Daniella and Dee decided they'd work on the anti-vampire spray. DeAnna and Deirdre were heading to the shop, and that left me on zombie hide-n-seek.

Which suited me fine. Although it meant that our search for Mariah Connors and her family line was postponed again. Part of me felt like it was no big deal. The other part of me felt like I had to find out something, get some kind of resolution because I had a date.

The thought struck me that I'd clawed my way out of Hell to find myself in a different sort of Hell. It wasn't just me, either. It was Deirdre and Daniella, and now Dee and DeAnna. Even Deana, who was sort of safely away.

If I died, if DeAnna was slated to die, or if those we loved were cursed to die—we'd be living in Hell on Earth.

Clever. My mind whirled with all the possibilities.

Eventually, I did what I did best. I put the worry about the curse to the side. I focused on finding out where the zombies were going. And I'd worry about what to wear around five tonight.

Mariah Connors and my potential return to Hell would need to wait.

"Done," I muttered. I looked over to see Beeval happily eating two pieces of chicken with bacon between them. "Beeval, be careful today."

He always ate our bait chicken, but hadn't seemed to have made the connection to Evil. I left it alone.

His big eyes turned to me. "Trouble? Demons?"

"No, zombies."

Beeval's nose wrinkled. "Smell. Waste of person."

"I could not agree more," I said. "But be careful. There's someone who is sending zombies out all over the place, and we don't know who he is."

"Grave robber," Beeval commented. "Scared men."

It amazed me how Beeval got to the heart of the matter. "You're right," I said. "And a scared man would be really happy to find you."

Beeval's eyes narrowed. "No one come here. I stop. Keep Evil safe." One hand reached up and patted Evil, who was sleeping on his head between his ears. While he ate chicken.

But then, we ate chicken as well. So maybe I was worrying over this too much.

"Thank you," I said, kneeling down to hug him. I got a one-armed hug in return, and I was careful to avoid bumping the chicken and bacon sandwich. "Tell Doc or Granny if someone comes snooping around."

"I blast," Beeval said. His eyes were hard.

Beeval was the cutest demon I'd ever met, but he went from cute to bad ass faster than you could speak the words. And I loved that. "Well, try not to kill him. Be low key."

Beeval looked up at me. "You want me to hold? Keep in place?"

I nodded. "If you can keep them out of the public eye."

Now it was Beeval's turn to nod. "I don't kill. Hold. Let you talk. Then kill."

"Perfect," I said. I hugged him again. "Be careful, OK?"

"I careful. I protect."

"I know you will." I stood up.

He patted my leg and went back to his sandwich. I watched him drift to the window, Evil still sleeping on his head. Inviting him here was one of the best things I'd ever done. I felt better, keeping him in the loop. He'd showed us that when we'd fought Ashlar. He was one of us.

Everyone went to get going on their tasks, and I drove to the shop with DeAnna and Deirdre. They'd agreed to man the shop, and I wanted to check on our basement houseguests.

I went directly to the basement. Note zombie was slumped against the bars, looking like whatever it was that kept him going had gotten up and left. I got chicken from the fridge, and tossed it into the cage. Three of them went for it.

Note zombie didn't move. This was so strange. I'd never seen a zombie just fall out like this. Although to be fair, we'd never kept them around this long. Normally, it was off with their head, and into a grave and an end to their suffering when they should be at peace. So maybe there wasn't anything nefarious about his losing steam.

I walked carefully around the cage. The other three zombies paid no attention to me, and I saw that the note was close to the bar.

I knelt down and moved slowly. My hand went in-between two bars. I got the piece of paper with my thumb and index finger and gently tugged.

It was pinned. Damn it all. It was pinned. I leaned down, twisting my head to see what kind of pin.

"A fucking straight pin," I whispered. "Are you kidding me?" Letting go of the note, I reached for the pin. When my fingers touched the metal of the pin, I got a zing that indicated magic. "Gotcha," I said, feeling victorious. Whatever this was, it had been put here deliberately. Ignoring the increasing pain from the pin,

I slid it out. The note stayed in place, which was totally gross to think about.

Letting the pin fall, I gently tugged at the note. The zombie didn't move, and I wondered if the magic I'd felt in the pin had kept him all snappy about this.

The note pulled away from his suit coat, and I finally got a look at it. The ink was written in a black marker which had faded, but was still legible. The paper itself was spelled. I could feel it through my fingers. Carefully, I picked up the pin, and holding the note with only two fingers, I went up to share my discovery.

DeAnna and Deirdre were at the counter.

"I got the note," I said.

"What note?" Deirdre asked. "Oh, the zombie note! Is there anything to it?"

I explained the magic I'd felt in the pin and paper.

"What does it say?" DeAnna asked. "The magic thing is weird."

I shook my head. "I don't know. It's just a series of numbers. And the magic means this is all deliberate, all planned." I showed them the note. The three of us looked at it, sitting on the counter. The numbers made no sense.

44 103
361 734
282 160

"That's not a spell, not that I know of," Deirdre frowned at the ragged piece of paper.

"We don't know that. People use all sorts of things for spell work," I objected.

"Thanks for the encouragement," Deirdre made a face. "Just what we need. An individualist."

"Well, who is most known for that?" DeAnna asked.

"Necromancers," I said.

"Mages," Deirdre said at the same time.

"Magic users who prefer to work alone," I said. "Witches tend to work together. We know the strength of working with many for one purpose. Mages and necromancers don't think that way."

Thinking about necromancers made me think of Zane, who hurried out of the car last night. Who was thinking about something other than our date last night —which was fine. We all had things to do. But it was more focused, like something had happened. Something that was pulling at his attention. I didn't want to think about what that could be. You know, just as we had a plague of zombies around the place. A thread of worry ran through me, and I just couldn't put it aside.

Zane wasn't telling me something he knew.

And that was a bad thing. I sighed. Was I trying to torpedo our date before it happened? I could see that. I would ask him. And see what he said. And do my best not to assume the worst.

Even as assuming the worst had kept me and my sisters alive for a long time. I sighed.

"I know," DeAnna said. "It's never ending, this protecting Deadwood business."

"This is busier than usual," Deirdre said.

"It is. You want to take a crack at this?" I asked Deirdre, gesturing at the note. "I want to get over to the gulch before tons of hikers are all over the place."

She nodded. "Abso-fuckin-lutely."

I could tell Deirdre was as pissed as I was about whoever this was making problems in our town. Which was good. Deirdre was the bulldog of the three of us. This joker, whoever he or she was, didn't stand a chance. Not in the long term.

Feeling better, I said, "All right. I'm off."

"Be careful," DeAnna said.

"Try not to die!" Deirdre yelled as I left. "You have a date tonight!"

"Well, if I'm gonna die, I get to be first," I said over my shoulder. "But I'll try to stay alive." I laughed, revving up the 911's engine in response. I knew they could hear me as I roared out of the alley.

There were some benefits to being able to live long enough to get the things you love. My Porsche 911 was one of them. Gunmetal gray, glossy, and fast as hell, it helped me burn off anger and frustration.

But as I was still in downtown Deadwood, I kept it under the speed limit. The current sheriff, named Everett Beauregard, loved giving me a ticket. I was, in his words, "an unrepentant repeat offender."

Whatevs. I had a 911 and he didn't. If I had to drive

their cars, I'd be bitter about other peoples' 911s, too. I'd made it through two months with no tickets, however, and I wanted to see how long I could keep the law-abiding streak going.

As I headed down the CanAm again, I kept my eyes open for any other shufflers while I debated where to stop so I could hike in. Hmmm. There was a camp-ground along the gulch just north of Deadwood Gulch, and a little lodge or something at the head of the gulch. There was nothing that would make this easy for me.

I sighed. Pulling into the parking lot for the camp-ground, I parked and grabbed the backpack I always kept in my car. I was wearing decent shoes for hiking, and I set out. I stopped at the lodge office, and asked the clerk, a woman named Marnie who was a regular customer at the tea shop, if I could hike down into the gulch.

"Are you looking for herbs?" Marnie asked, looking up from the book she was reading.

I nodded. "Maybe. One of our customers told me she saw a plant that I've been looking for." This would give me a good cover story should anyone ask.

After so many years of chasing shit in and around Deadwood, I was always prepared. I didn't keep only a stocked backpack in the car—I'd also grabbed my trekking poles. In addition to keeping me from falling on my ass, they had a wicked sharp end that was perfect for poking things that were coming at one. This worked even better as I'd filed them a bit to sharpen them further.

You know, the whole being prepared thing.

"Well, go on. Good luck!" Marnie smiled, clearly eager to return to her book. I waved and walked across the parking lot, intending to hike over the hill and down into Deadwood Gulch.

As I stepped into the trees, I stopped, letting myself take several deep breaths, enjoying the scent of the trees. I let my magic go free, washing over me like a cool breeze, feeling it coil in my fingertips, and ready itself in my body. We Nightingales tended to be pretty all or nothing with our spells, but it had worked well for the past hundred years. If it wasn't broke, don't fix it, was my motto.

Although I'd be interested in talking with Zane about how he did spells, since he studied with—no! I shook my head. I wasn't interested in doing anything with Zane for the time being. I'd already noodled on that too much. No. I pushed the thought of Zane away. Thinking about him meant I'd start thinking about what he wasn't telling me.

Magic at the ready, I started hiking up the hill. According to the map, I'd need to get over this hill, and I'd be down in Deadwood Gulch, and see if my gut instinct was right, or if it was completely off base. It felt good to be up in the hills, surrounded by trees, with no people.

I crested the hill and began the descent into the

gulch. There was no development here, no houses, no nothing. Not now, anyway. Around the time we were born, there had been mining here, as there was everywhere in Deadwood that people could make a claim. The town had changed

As I got to the bottom of the gulch, and headed south along the bottom, I walked past a heap of old, weathered timbers.

My fingers tingled, and I felt a shift in my stomach. Like that feeling before you drop down an elevator, like you felt when you were a kid on a slide. Stopping, I all but held my breath.

Then I heard it.

A shuffling in the trees, in the leaves and pine needles that had fallen. I looked around, trying to figure out where the noise was coming from. I heard it again, and it was coming from my left. I crouched down, looking for something to hide behind. There wasn't much.

I ducked back behind a tree, hoping that the person wouldn't look too closely.

From my semi-hiding place, I watched as the steps got closer, and louder. A zombie came past me, looking neither left nor right, intent on whatever was in front of him.

All I needed to do now was follow him.

I let him shuffle by, trying hold as still as possible. This poor schlub didn't have a chance against me, but I didn't want to have to fight with him. The only people I picked fight with were my family and demons. The thought made me smile.

The zombie headed off further south, his clothes catching on trees. The small tugs at his sleeves and pants—an outfit that looked like it came from the forties, and my man was pretty skeletal looking, which made me wonder how no one had called the cops on this dude—made no difference to him. He was intent on wherever it was he was headed. After I waited a minute—I counted to sixty—I went after him.

He wasn't being quiet, wasn't even trying to be quiet.

I followed along, looking to either side of me as I walked. I tried to step carefully. Thank Goddess this zombie wasn't fast.

But he was focused, and he kept going. Getting back up the hill to my car was going to be a bitch.

Without warning, the air in front of the zombie shimmered. I stopped and crouched down again.

The zombie walked on through the shimmer. OK, that was weird. And suspect. No damn zombie set that whatever it was. But normal air didn't shimmer.

Watching the zombie, he kept on in the same direction, like that shimmer wasn't even there.

Well, all right then. I stood up, and walked to the shimmer. Taking a breath, I made to walk through it.

And got knocked on my ass, about five feet backward from the shimmer.

"Shit," I swore, scrambling backwards like a crab, my trekking poles splayed out, trying to get into the cover of a tree or shrub. If the person who set this was smart, and I had to think they were, they'd have some kind of alarm when someone non-zombie hit their shimmer wall. I didn't want to be seen.

When I peeked out around from the tree where I'd backed up to, I couldn't see the zombie anymore. Damn it all to hell. I'd lost him. But I knew where he was.

I wasn't ready to move, though. I wanted to make sure that no one came looking to see who had tried to get through their wall.

My magic tingled, and I sent a shot of light from my right hand, wanting to see what happened. The golden light hit the shimmer. There was a ripple across the shimmer. The magic from my little light dart kept on going, and I could see that the shimmer went across the length of the gulch.

This was not good.

Someone had decided to squat in my city, and that shit didn't fly. The anger at the nerve of whoever this was flared up again, and I could feel my magic swirling, ready for another go.

But that wasn't the smart idea. I needed to get back to the house, talk with my sisters and nieces, and tackle this as a family.

I sighed, taking breaths and forcing my magic to stand down.

After thirty minutes, and having seen no one, not even another zombie, I pushed myself backwards more, and then moved back toward the head of the gulch and the road. I kept looking over my shoulder, letting my magic hang at the ready, so to speak. If some joker came after me, I'd show him or her what it felt like to be knocked on your ass.

But my preparation was for nothing. I hiked back up the hill, and down to the RV campground where I'd left my car, remembering to shove some herbs into my bag in case Marnie saw me again.

Sometimes it was tough to always have to have a cover story, but that was part of being a Nightingale.

I tossed my backpack and poles into the car, and headed home, waving at the office as I drove away in case anyone was looking.

I needed to get home and tell my sisters about this.

Someone *was* on our turf, and they'd gone to some trouble to hide themselves. And that was before we even got to the subject of the zombies that passed through with no problem. It was a barrier designed to keep out the living.

And that shit didn't fly in Deadwood.

CHAPTER EIGHT

I didn't really want to go to the shop, because I hated to bring bad news.

Parking out back, I saw that the work truck and the Jeep were still there. That was good—nothing had happened to make Deirdre close up. I came through the back to see Deirdre and DeAnna at the front counter, talking to two women. Dealing with customers was not what I wanted, so I changed course and veered left into our small office.

Within minutes, they both came in.

"Well?" Deirdre asked.

"You look sweaty and hot," DeAnna said.

"I am," I pulled the hair off my neck, twisting it into a messy bun and sticking a pencil from the desk through it. "I could really use water, too."

Neither of them moved.

"Fine," I muttered, heading out of the office to get

water from the fridge. I walked back to the office, drinking right from the bottle.

"What did you find?" DeAnna asked.

"Well, someone with good magical warding skills has set up shop in our backyard," I said. "Whoever they are, they are good."

"What the hell?" Deirdre asked, her eyebrows raised. "That's some balls. Everyone knows we're here."

"It's like they're asking for trouble," DeAnna said.

"Or they need to be here and are just trying to fly under the Nightingale radar," I said.

"What kind of ward?" Deirdre got down to business.

"I don't know what kind of spell, but it makes a shimmer."

"What do you mean, a shimmer?" DeAnna asked.

"It's a ward, but it wasn't invisible," I said.

"Amateur," Deirdre sniffed.

"Yeah, but it was strong," I said. "I tried to get through, and it knocked me backwards."

"Like, on your ass?" Deirdre looked like she was trying to hide a grin.

"I would have liked to have seen that," DeAnna added.

"Yes, on my ass," I rolled my eyes. "Whatever it was, it was strong."

"And you could see it?" DeAnna moved right from teasing to thoughtful. "That's interesting. Either he or she didn't even try to hide it, or they couldn't."

We had a lot of experience with hiding wards.

DeAnna had cause to have seen them in action, what with Ashlar trying to off us all. In the past month, we'd had to do a couple over the town. Demons showing up on your front lawn had that affect.

I shook my head. "I don't know."

"Was it to stop you?"

"The zombie I was following—"

"You didn't mention a zombie!" Deirdre interrupted.

"I didn't?" I pushed my hair away from my face. I was still hot. "Well, I hiked over into Deadwood Gulch from the RV place, you know the one?" I looked at them, and Deirdre nodded. "And when I got down into the gulch, I just walked along the bottom. I heard some kind of shuffling, and big as day, there was a zombie, heading on down the gulch like he was out for a stroll."

"Anyone we recognize?" Deirdre asked.

"No. He was old, like from the forties. There was bone showing. I don't know how no one called *that* in," I said.

"And then?" DeAnna asked.

"He walked through the shimmer. I tried to follow him and was blocked."

"On your ass," Deirdre smiled briefly.

"Yes. We've established that. Who would have the balls to set up shop here?"

"Well, Deadwood Gulch down there is a good place. There's no one there. No trails, no nothing." Deirdre was tapping her lip.

"Is there anything there anymore?" I asked.

Deirdre shook her head.

"Old cabins? Mine sites? Abandoned houses? Caves?" I persisted. "I can't believe we don't know!" We knew Deadwood in and out. Or at least, I thought we did.

"That's been unused or occupied for a long time. No need for us to know," Deirdre replied. "Not worth beating ourselves up for."

I sighed, leaning back in the chair. "You're right. I hate not knowing."

"Well, we still need to be here for a couple more hours," DeAnna said.

I looked at my watch. She was right. It was long after lunch.

"Is there anything to eat?"

"You could get us a burger," Deirdre said.

"Saloon No. 10 it is," I said, getting up. I would never say no to a Crab Hollandaise burger. Not ever. Not even were I close to death. That was one of those things that was a fixed point for me. If they ever went out of business, I think a part of me might shrivel up and die.

Even as I knew I'd be there later tonight. Well, I'd be in the restaurant. Not the bar, where I normally went.

I went down to the saloon and ordered lunch, taking the time to talk with Duffy, the bartender. While we made small talk, I saw some of the ghosts lingering around.

Normally, I ignored them, and they ignored me. I'd known some of them when they were alive, and apparently, there had been a lot of gossip because of Doc. All reasons to keep a polite distance. Today, however, I could feel them hovering.

"Duffy, I'll be right back," I said.

She nodded from down the bar, and I made my way to the bathrooms. They were down a long, narrow, dark hallway. I also knew there was a supply closet back there, and bypassing the restrooms, I went into the closet, closing the door behind me as I turned on the light.

"All right, what is it? I can feel you guys."

Two ghosts appeared. I was right. They'd wanted to talk. A man named Gordie and a woman named Nadine. Both were from the late 1800s, as their clothing showed.

"I'm so glad you came in," Nadine said. "It's been a while, and we've been keeping a look out."

"What's up?" I asked. This wasn't good.

"There's trouble," Gordie said.

"All kinds," I replied. "What do you know?"

"There's someone bringing back the dead. But not our dead," Nadine said.

"You're sure about that?" I asked.

"You don't look surprised," Gordie said, crossing his arms.

"We've been dealing with the zombies," I said shortly.

Nadine crossed herself. "May they rest in peace."

"There's someone bad here who's bringing them in,"

Gordie said, repeating what Nadine had said. "They're not from around here, and whoever he is—"

"You know it's a he?" I asked.

"That's what we hear," Gordie said.

"From who?" I asked.

"Some of those poor people have their spirits with them still," Nadine said.

"Can I talk to one of them?" I asked. This could solve a lot of problems.

Gordie shook his head. "We haven't really talked to them. They move in passing. It's different," he said, seeing me getting ready to ask more questions. "We're at peace in some ways. We choose to be here. But these poor bastards—they aren't at peace, and are being used against their will."

"For what?"

Nadine said, "They're very scattered, all over the place," her hands fluttered. "But they are digging."

"Digging?" That made no sense. "Like mining?" We had a strong mining history here, but other than the Wharf mine west of here, there was no active mining. Even the Homestake mine, which had operated for over one hundred years, had shut down.

"They're digging for something," Gordie said. "They don't know what. They dig, and they rest."

"That makes no sense, but it's something I didn't know. Thank you," I said.

"We don't need this here," Nadine said, sounding very prim.

"You're right. We don't. Thank you," I said again. "Is there anything else you know?"

They both shook their heads.

"We don't really see many of them," Nadine said. "But a few have drifted through here, and then they leave. I don't think they wanted to," she said, looking away from me.

"What do you mean?" I asked.

"It's as though they are taken away," Gordie said. "They're not in control of their spirits, either."

"None of that points to someone with good intentions," I said.

"No, ma'am, it does not," Gordie said. "We'll send word if we hear more."

"Get word to Doc if I don't come in," I said, opening the door. "I appreciate you telling me this. You can let the others know we're on it."

Both the ghosts faded away. I slipped out of the room, bumping into two women.

"Are you all right, honey?" The older one asked.

"Went in the wrong door," I pasted a smile on my face. "I thought this was the bathroom."

They both smiled, and I moved past them and back to the bar.

"It's all ready," Duffy smiled at me. She pushed a bag across the bar.

I signed the check and got myself out of there. Back at the shop, after I shared the message from the Saloon No. 10 ghosts, the three of us ate and everyone ignored the zombie in the middle of the room, so to speak, choosing to talk about the spray for Deana.

Which, had this been a normal early summer day, would have been a fun way to spend the next couple of days. I loved creating. I wondered how we could market this. We couldn't say it kept vampires away— but would it work on other beings? Humans? Something to think about. We had the shop, and all of us had invested, so we did well financially, but I was always on the lookout to find things that would keep income flowing for us.

I went and checked on our zombies. We'd need to put them to rest tonight. The one who I'd taken the note from was on the floor, and not moving at all. He'd slid down from where I'd seen him this morning. If we left him much longer, the other zombies would have a go at him, and I didn't want that.

We knew where they were headed. The ghosts confirmed what our graveyard patrol had already discovered—these weren't Deadwood folks. So it was time.

As I climbed the stairs, I thought about how to manage this. Normally, it was only the three or four of us. There were five of us, plus Zane—

Shit. I couldn't do it tonight. I had a date.

"We need to put them to rest," I said to Deirdre and DeAnna quietly. There were customers in the shop.

"What? Now?" Deirdre whirled around. "Because we don't have enough going on?"

"Note guy is out. Stretched out on the floor. Whatever was holding him together isn't there anymore."

Deirdre sighed. I didn't have to explain it to her. "We can go tonight."

"I can't," I said.

"What—oh, that's right. No, you can't. And we won't let you, will we, DeAnna?"

DeAnna shook her head. "No way, missy. You're not missing your date."

They both grinned at me.

I threw up my hands. "Fine. I know you all can handle it."

"Oh, blessed by the great Desdemona," Deirdre intoned, rolling her eyes. "Such praise."

"Shut up," I said. "Give me something to do. I can't go home yet. I'll go crazy."

"Go find some herbs that may work for the spray," Deirdre said. "Then go home and see if you can help Dee and Daniella. We're on a deadline for Deana."

"Please," DeAnna said. "Dee's going crazy."

"And you're not?" I teased.

"I have great faith in my granddaughter," DeAnna said proudly. "She's the strongest of the three of us."

"She was," I said. "You two are evening the playing field."

DeAnna looked surprised, and then pleased. "Thank you," she said. Her cheeks pinked at the praise. "Go, Desdemona. Go see what you can find, and then go help her."

I nodded, and went to the storeroom. It took me an hour to pull things I thought might work, but I bagged up the herbs in sample bags, and went back out to the front of the shop. "All right. I'm headed out."

I drove home, thinking about the spray. Vampires weren't alive, which kind of threw a lot of normal herb lore. But I thought we might have a solution, particularly if it was combined with some Nightingale magic.

When I pulled into the garage at Pearl street, I went straight the basement stillroom. Dee and Daniella looked up.

"Well?" Daniella asked.

I gave them the updates, and told them about the ward set up in Deadwood Gulch. As I expected, that pissed of Daniella as well.

"Nervy bastard."

"The ghosts think it's a he."

"What?" Dee asked, confusion in her expression.

I told them about meeting Nadine and Gordie.

Daniella sighed. "This all points to a necromancer, Des."

"Or a mage," I said.

"OK, could be a mage, too. But necros like zombie help."

Now it was my turn to sigh. "Yes, they do. I have more good news," I said.

"Why do I think you don't have good news at all?" Dee asked, her lips curving up a little.

"You're learning," Daniella said.

"The zombies need to be put to rest tonight. One of them is down—the one with the note," I added.

"Did you get the note?"

"I did," I said, and told them about that.

"Good grief," Dee said. "There is so much to take in."

"When this kind of thing hits, it all tends to be related," I said. "The thing with Ashlar? And then the curse? All related to Granny. I'd bet this is all related too, and we just haven't seen it."

"Take off the tinfoil," Daniella said. She didn't concur with my general thoughts that everything usually ended up tied together.

Even though they did, and I was usually right.

"I have no idea what the note means, although Deirdre is working on it. But the zombies need to go. One's down, and you know that's a bad sign for the rest of them. Plus, it will mean so much cleaning for us," I said.

"Oh Goddess, yes. Too much cleaning," Daniella said. "OK, we'll get the zombies back in the ground tonight. You're not going near it."

"I know, I know. The date. But that's not for a couple of hours. I have some ideas for the spray."

"We're open," Dee said. "We've put together a few things, and they don't even knock me out."

"You're testing on Dee?" I turned on Daniella.

"Well, they need to be tested. Dee's fine."

"Are you fine?" I looked back at Dee.

"Yes. Although I've been struck with a need to go to the bathroom more," Dee replied.

"Too much dandelion," Daniella said.

"And that was part of it why?" I asked. "No, don't," I said, holding up a hand. "Listen, vampires are dead, right?"

"As far as we know," Daniella said.

"So a lot of the things we'd use to affect the body are based on the body being alive. Vamps aren't really alive, and their body functions don't work like a human's anymore."

"Right," Dee said.

"What do they do that we do?" I asked.

"What? Oh, sleep!" Daniella said.

I nodded. "An enhanced sleeping potion. One that is temporary, but immediate. Knock out spray. So if you needed to get away from one, you'd spray them, and have the time to haul ass."

"It would need to be as much time as possible," Daniella said. Her eyes were unfocused, which meant she was turning the lists of herbs over in her mind.

"But not too much," I argued. "We don't want them waking up and missing tons of time. Or getting caught in the sunlight. It needs to be seen as something a clever human thought up, but not enough to set their pride totally on fire."

"Good thought," Daniella said.

"What does their pride have to do with it?" Dee asked.

"They're very proud, and have huge egos. You offend them, and that's like the worst thing ever. You get one over on them because of cleverness, you have a better chance of not being dinner."

"Or turned," Daniella said. She saw Dee's face, and reached out for our niece. "I don't think that's going to happen to Deana. They know who she is. They know she's one of us. They know we'd pull up stakes and ruin them, if they hurt her."

"Do they?" Dee's lip trembled.

I nodded. "They do. We've only had to pick a fight out of Deadwood once, and we won. Even without the power of Deadwood behind us, we won."

"You'll have to tell me about it," Dee said. She still looked upset.

"Later. Let's get to work on this," I said. I knew she needed, having used the technique for myself many times. She needed to keep busy.

By five-thirty, we had a mixture that we felt had promise. I wanted to try it out, but Daniella and Dee sent me upstairs to get ready.

"Because you stink," Daniella said.

I didn't dignify her insult with an answer, and went to shower. Once I got out, after spending longer than normal in the shower, I went to my closet. I had no idea what to wear. I hadn't had a date in decades. I wore clothing for whatever we were dealing with, which usually included jeans, boots, and a tee shirt.

Which is all Zane had seen me in.

Did I want him to see me differently? I didn't know. He already saw something in me—and I had to admit, I wanted to see those eyes light up when he looked at me.

Moving the hangers along the rod, I found a black dress toward the back. It was a sleeveless sundress kind of thing, and it had a little sweater that went with it. That would cover most of the burn marks that looked like weird tattoos that were on my arms and part of my neck and collarbone area. "Thanks, asshole," I said without heat, thinking about what I'd had to do to get out of hell. That's where the burn marks had come from.

Back to clothes. Black flats—I didn't like heels, because it was hard to run in them if you needed to—and some jewelry, and I'd be good. I'd look somewhat different from my daily garb.

I took time drying my hair, noting all the red that was in it. When I'd escaped from Hell, my hair had taken on red and amber highlights. I found that I liked it. I left my hair down, letting the natural wave do its thing. I put on a little makeup, but not much. Again, it wasn't my thing.

Gold hoop earrings, a gold necklace with a locket that had a picture of Meema in it, and I was ready.

I took a breath. My heart was beating faster than normal. I looked at my phone. It was six thirty-seven. I had enough time to get downtown and find parking. Since it was summer, the restaurants were starting to get busier.

As I walked into the main kitchen area, my sisters and Dee and DeAnna were sitting around the table.

"You look great," Deirdre said.

"Have fun," Dee said. She smiled.

Doc materialized. "Darlin', you'll knock his socks off."

"I'm not sure that's what I want," I said in a moment of complete honesty.

"Whatever it is you want, you can have it," he said quietly, his hand brushing my cheek like a focused breeze.

"Thanks," I said.

"You look hot," Daniella said. "He's going to cry when he sees you."

It was the right thing to say, to remind me that no matter what, I was a Nightingale.

"I have to go," I said. I escaped down the stairs to the garage, revving the 911 out onto the street.

It didn't take long to get downtown, but parking was more a challenge, and I walked into the door of Saloon No. 10's restaurant side with three minutes to spare.

"Hi, Desdemona," Tasha, the hostess said. "Your friend is already here." She smiled, and turned to lead me to a table.

Zane stood up as we got close. He pulled out a chair, and pushed it in as I sat down.

"Your waiter will be right over," Tasha said. She smiled again, and disappeared.

"You look beautiful," Zane said.

"So do you," I looked over at him. He was wearing a black suit, with a black shirt, and black tie. I found that I liked the all black look on him. It made his eyes stand out even more.

Speaking of which, I looked right into his eyes, and I saw admiration, and desire, and... a warmth pooled into my midsection.

Oh, holy hell.

CHAPTER NINE

We talked quietly, as Zane asked me about how things had gone in Deadwood Gulch. When I told him about the ward that stretched across the gulch, and then the note that I'd gotten off the zombie, along with the magic that I'd felt—his face darkened.

"What do you know?" I asked.

Zane sighed. "I really didn't want to talk about this tonight. Could we table it for a little while?"

"I guess. Tell me about how you grew up," I said.

"That's another mess," Zane said.

I turned to face him. "Something's up with that," I said. "I've noticed that something is off with you, and I feel like you're not telling me something. I mean," I realized that I was in full-on interrogation mode, "Your life is your business. I respect that, appearances notwithstanding."

He smiled a little, and I felt the tension between us lighten up.

"But if you know something about what's going on, and honestly, it's looking like a necromancer is involved, this is where you have to take a stand, Zane. I know it's got to be hard, but if you really want to live here, want to live where there are rules, and people that see the rules are followed," I was quoting, sort of, something he'd said to me when I asked him why he wanted to be here, "Then you have to be on the side of the rules and the people who make sure they're followed."

Zane looked at me with those green eyes, and then looked away, leaning forward on the table on his clasped hands.

Shit. This wasn't good. "What?" I asked, leaning closer to him. I put my hand on his arm. "Zane, we're on the same side. We're all on your side."

"You are?" He looked at me, and his eyes looked bleak. "Even though I'm a necromancer?"

"When I told my family we were having dinner, the whole house burst out cheering."

He smiled, the look in his eyes lightening. "Really?"

I nodded.

"I would have liked to have seen that."

"It was something," I mumbled, feeling my face heat at the memory.

"That makes me feel good. I really like you. I always have," he said.

"Even when I nearly blasted you when you came at me in the bar?" I asked, smiling.

"Even then. I could feel the magic swirling around you."

"Why'd you continue, then?"

He shrugged. "I really do like Doc, and I like the idea of helping souls move on, if that's what they want."

"Where did you learn that?" I asked. "I know that's not how you were raised."

His face shuttered then.

I sat back, surprised. It was like watching someone close a door right in front of you. But I kept quiet, wanting to see what he'd say.

Our dinner arrived then, and we both focused on our meals for a few moments. After he'd taken a couple of bites, Zane took a long drink of his wine, and looked directly at me. "Remember I told you that I'd broken my ties with my father?"

I nodded, drinking my own wine.

"It was because he tried to bring my mother back."

"What?" I whispered. "Why?"

"He thought she had information he wanted. She was a witch," he smiled, lifting his glass at me. "My dad fell hard for her, and she apparently fell for him as well. But she died, and it was though part of the good in him died with her. He stopped caring about the cost of what he did. It was all about what he wanted. That was the only thing he took into consideration. And he decided that she had information he needed, and he went to her grave, and he brought her back."

"Oh, my Goddess," I said, putting my hand over my mouth. "How did you find out?"

"I walked into his workroom, and there she was," Zane looked over his wineglass, and I knew that he was back in that workroom. "I yelled at him, asking what the hell he was doing, and he didn't even look up from where he was writing, and told me to either help, or go away."

He fell silent.

I kept silent. This needed no conversation from me.

"I said, Why is she here? And he said, That's my business. You can help, or get out. He didn't even look at me. So I turned, as though I was going to go back to the house, and I grabbed an axe that was next to the door, and I took three steps—they felt like the longest steps I'd ever taken—and I chopped off her head." His voice had dropped to a whisper.

It was as though the restaurant had faded away, and it was just me and Zane sitting together. I reached across and took his hand. "I am so sorry," I said.

He looked at me then, and I could see the shimmer of tears in his eyes. "I never thought, in all the crazy shit I'd done, and might have to do, that sending my mother back to her death was going to be one of them." He threaded his fingers through mine, and placed his other hand on top. As though he needed the reassurance of touch.

This, I got. Sometimes you had to do things that felt horrible. And you questioned your very humanity. In all my years, however, I'd never had to do what Zane had done.

"As you can imagine, my father paid attention to me then. He came at me, and punched me in the face. All the while, he was yelling, calling me a stupid boy, telling me I didn't know what I'd done—and I yelled back, telling him that I'd allowed my mother to rest as she deserved to. Then he slapped me, and told me to get out of his house."

Zane looked at me. "Until then, I didn't think much of raising zombies. I felt like they were a useful tool and that was all I thought. When I saw my mother, rotting from the grave, I realized what they were, what we were doing. What we were. We were monsters." He looked down.

"What did you do then?" I asked.

"I went to my mother's best friend. Her name was Kyra, she's a witch. I told her everything, and told her I didn't want to be like my father, and I asked her how to escape what seemed like my only path at that time. She let me cry, and then she told me that she'd show me another way. I was with her for five more years before I went out on my own."

"How old were you when you left your father's house?" I asked.

"Sixteen," he said. "I left Kyra's when I was twenty-one. I travelled, and helped with magical messes when I could. I heard of Deadwood, and how you three—well, four, then—kept things on the straight and narrow, and how you didn't put up with anyone's shit. And I knew that's the kind of place I wanted to be. Somewhere where things were clear. Black and white."

I squeezed his hand. Zane always seemed so calm, so controlled. This was raw and honest.

We finished dinner, and when he'd paid the bill, Zane turned to me. "You want to go for a walk? I know you live here, but I want to pretend, just for tonight, that this is a normal date."

I stood up, smiling. "This is a normal date."

He smiled, and as he stood, he took my hand.

I let him. We walked out into the night, holding hands. It felt... nice.

Something had shifted for me when he told me about himself. He didn't have to reveal that, but he'd chosen to.

"Is that what's been bothering you?" I asked, not looking at him. "That this is like your dad?"

"This is exactly like my dad. Using zombies, not really caring about who might get hurt—whoever is doing this knows what they're doing, and they are focused on that, without care for anyone else."

"We're going to stop him," I said.

"I'm counting on it," Zane squeezed my hand.

I felt the warmth flow through me, and I wanted to be closer to him, but I restrained myself. This now surpassed when Marcus Gibby had taken my hand over one hundred years ago. I was so busy thinking that I wasn't paying attention to what was in front of me.

"Dammit!" I shouted as I tripped. I braced myself for falling on my face.

But I didn't. A pair of strong arms, attached to very nice, shapely shoulders, caught me.

"Thanks," I said, turning only a little to look at Zane.

His green(???) eyes regarded me in a way that made me feel warm all over.

"I don't mind catching you," Zane said.

"I'm not used to having anyone that catches," I said.

"Your sisters do," he replied.

"That's not the same," I said, not willing to pretend tonight.

As if time slowed down, I saw his head getting closer to mine. I was mesmerized by the green of his eyes, eyes that looked into mine as though there was nothing else in the world right now but him, and me.

Then his lips came down on mine. A burst of desire, and of something else I couldn't identify raced through me, as though I'd touched a live electrical wire. But in a good way. In a really, really good way .

Holy shit, I thought. I've never felt that before. And I've kissed a lot of lips, truth be told.

Then Zane pulled away, and I was standing up, blinking as though I'd woken from a wonderful dream.

"I'll always catch you," he whispered. "You just have to let me."

I ran a hand through my hair, not sure how to respond. "Kiss me again," I said.

He didn't hesitate. He leaned down, capturing my lips, and right there, on the streets of my hometown where I'd spent over one hundred years trying not to be seen as anything other than a nice girl with interesting hobbies, I kissed Zane McAllister. He kissed me back. It was the best thing that had happened to me in a long time.

When we finally parted as someone walked around us, we were both breathless. Zane took my hand, and in silent agreement, walked back toward the parking lot.

"I'd ask you to come back to my place, but I think it's too soon," Zane said.

"I think you're right," I said, feeling a little shy, as well as pleased that he wanted to invite me back to his place.

"So why don't I walk you to your car, and we'll get back into the protecting Deadwood business tomorrow?" Zane asked. I could hear the smile in his words.

"I can agree with that."

We walked to my car, and as I unlocked it, I found that I wasn't sure how to say good night. I turned around, and he took me in his arms, kissing me again, but without some of the heat from our earlier kiss. I realized that he was holding back.

Which was a good thing. I felt like I was about to go up in flames at his touch.

Zane let me go. "You have to make me a promise, though."

"What?" I was breathless again.

"We go out again in three days. No matter what, Desdemona."

"OK. Three days," I said. I felt like I would have agreed to anything he said at that moment. His lips were like magic.

He kissed my forehead and then reached around me to open my car door. "Don't speed," he said.

I laughed, feeling a little more normal then. Only a little. But he knew about my ticket problem. "I won't."

"See you tomorrow," Zane said, and closed the door behind me after I got in.

I drove home with the biggest smile on the planet all over my face. When I pulled into the garage, I took a moment to try and compose myself, but it was hard. I hadn't felt this good in... I couldn't remember how long.

Slowly, I walked up the stairs. As I came into the kitchen, I saw that the four of them were around the table, all working on laptops.

Everyone looked up as I came in.

"How did it—never mind," DeAnna said, smiling. "I don't even need to ask. Your smile gives it all away."

"What smile?" I asked.

"That one," Daniella got up. She was wearing pajamas, and I looked at everyone else.

They were all in pajamas.

"Did you get all of them moved?" I asked.

Dee grimaced. "Yes, and you didn't warn us strongly enough how messy it is."

"I'm sorry," I said. Now I could feel the smile.

"No, you're not, but that's all right. I'm thinking of it as a baptism in nasty," Dee said.

Everyone laughed.

"That's a perfect way to describe it," I said. "A baptism in nasty."

"Hence strong showers and PJs," DeAnna said. "But they're in the ground, poor things."

"So how did it go?" Daniella asked.

"Wonderful."

"He is still our friend? You haven't scared him away?" Deirdre teased.

"We have a date in three days," I said without thinking.

There was silence, and then my sisters and my nieces all surrounded me, hugging me. They were happy for me, and I realized, in that moment, how stuck we were. How glad I was that Zane had insisted on moving to Pearl street, how glad I was that I'd met him.

Because this was how we'd handle the next hundred years.

By moving forward.

I hugged all of my sisters, since that was what Dee and DeAnna were becoming, and went to bed. I wanted to bask in the nice evening before the realities of the day hit.

I fell asleep with a smile on my face.

CHAPTER TEN

The next morning, I was still smiling when I woke. It was early, and I made breakfast for everyone. We talked about the vampire spray, and since it was still early, we all trooped downstairs to the still-room to try out the new ideas.

It was Monday, which meant that the shop was closed. We worked through lunch, and finally, Daniella and Deirdre spelled our latest mixture.

"We need to test it," I said.

Whatever anyone was going to say was interrupted by a banging on the door upstairs.

"What the hell?" Deirdre muttered.

The three of us ran lightly up the stairs, focusing our magic as we ran. I went to the door and opened it to find Zane.

He leaned against the door jam, breathing heavily.

"What's wrong?" I asked, panic blooming through me.

"A zombie," he said. "I have it in my garage. I went to the shop and you weren't there."

"Where'd you find the zombie?" Daniella asked.

"Is today the one day you weren't listening to the police scanner?" he asked.

"No, we were in the stillroom all morning," I said.

Zane looked at me, and then held up a hand. "You'll tell me later. There was a call about a raggedy man at the Olaf Seim mine site, and the woman was worried he'd fall in one of the old shafts."

"You have a scanner?" I asked. "After you gave me grief?"

Zane grinned, and I remembered how it felt to have those lips on mine. I grinned back. I couldn't help it.

"Seemed like a good idea, you know, to keep up with what's going on. You mean I got the drop on the Nightingales?"

"We're kind of busy here," Daniella said.

"Why didn't you come and get us?"

"I can handle zombies," Zane said, and I heard the thread of steel in his voice.

"You can," I agreed.

He smiled at me as our eye met, and for a moment, it was just the two of us.

"Snap out of it!" Deirdre said. "We need you two on task, not on the moon."

"Sorry," I said. "You're right. We need to get him out of your garage. What was he doing up there at the mine?"

"Digging," Zane said.

"Just like the ghosts said," I breathed.

Deirdre sighed. "Let's get him to the shop," she said.

"Get who?" Dee asked. She and DeAnna had come up.

"Another zombie," Daniella said.

"We could test the spray on him!" DeAnna said.

We all looked at her.

"Well, zombies aren't alive. Just like vampires, right?" She looked around. "What? They're both dead."

"You are brilliant," I said.

"Because she's a Nightingale," Deirdre said.

"And a Holliday," Doc's voice chimed in from the kitchen.

"And a Holliday," I agreed. "Which is a double whammy."

In short order, I went with Zane to get the zombie down to the shop, and the rest took Deirdre's Jeep, planning to meet us down there with the spray. We could test it on the zombie, on each other, and time it, and then if it was good, make up a large batch and get it out to Deana tomorrow.

Zane took my hand as we walked to his place, and I let him.

He had a truck with a cap on it, and I could see the

zombie bumping around. It was a lot more lively than the last ones we'd had.

That was a mystery that I hadn't figured out yet. In all my years, I'd never heard of zombies winding down.

"Good call, getting him in here," I said.

"Well, it's kind of a family tradition, sadly," Zane replied. "I thought when I moved here my zombie wrangling was behind me."

"Anything can happen in Deadwood," I said.

"Clearly. Now what is this spray, and why do you need to test it?"

As we drove to the shop, I filled him in on the call from Deana, and her need to be able to get away from vampires in a hurry.

"They won't be happy when they wake up," Zane said.

"No, but when are they ever happy?" I shrugged. "Humans, even witch humans, need all the advantages they can get with vampires. They're so damn fast, it's hard to go against them even with magic."

"That's true," he agreed.

As we pulled into the back of the shop, everyone was waiting. Daniella had chicken out before we even got out of the truck.

"Get ready with the stasis spells," I said. "He's a lively one."

Dee's nose wrinkled. "Great."

Zane opened up the tailgate as I opened up the cap's top, and the zombie rushed out, making us all jump back. Daniella waved the chicken, and the zombie stilled, and then began moving toward her.

With Deirdre and I ready to zap him, Daniella got him down to the cage. I breathed a sigh of relief when the door clanged shut behind him.

"I don't like these zombies," I said. "They're not normal."

"No, they're not," Zane said. "They are spelled for sure."

"Why was he digging?" DeAnna asked.

"What is the master looking for?" Zane asked.

"That's the question," I said. "What is the master looking for? It doesn't matter who it is. I think we can agree that he's not a good guy."

"We're going with the ghost intel that it's a he?" Deirdre asked.

"They're usually pretty good with intel," I said. "But even if they're shaky on details, they're worried. So yes, I'll go with that. Doesn't it feel like it's a he?"

Daniella nodded. So did Deirdre.

"I think it's a necromancer," Zane said.

"We agree with you," I said. "All right, let's test this stuff on our friend here."

Dee handed me the spray bottle. We'd come up with a mixture of lavender, valerian root, passion flower, and tryptophan. Then we'd added a strong enhancement spell to it. If we were right, this should knock the zombie out.

I walked to where the zombie was leaning against

the bar. He snapped his teeth at me. I sprayed him in the face.

He stilled, and then snapped his teeth again.

"Give it another spray," Daniella said.

I sprayed him again, and he stopped, mouth half open, arm reaching for me.

"He really should be dropping," Dee said. "This won't help her get away."

"One more," I said, and I sprayed him a third time.

The zombie stilled again, and then slumped against the bars.

I leaned in and poked at him.

"Hey!" Deirdre yelled. "Don't do that!"

I poked at his shoulder, and he slid down the bar further. "He's out. Did someone start the timer?"

We spent another hour allowing the zombie to wake, only to spray him again. Then, after we reproduced the same times for him being out—around seven minutes—we took turns spraying one another.

Which was just as hilarious as it sounded. Finally, DeAnna sprayed us all, and timed it.

It worked on humans, although only around three minutes. A little more than that, but three minutes was a safe bet.

"Let's go make a huge batch of this," I said, feeling happier about the situation in Deadwood than I'd felt since the zombies started showing up. "I think this will really help Deana, but we need to have some of this for ourselves."

"I'm already carrying the spell bags," DeAnna said. "I'm going to look silly with all these things in my pockets."

We'd made spell bags for Dee, Deana, and DeAnna when Dee and Deana went back east to meet with a necromancer who had the angel sword we needed. I knew that Deana carried hers, but I didn't know that DeAnna was still carrying hers. The spell bags would let them cast fire and stasis spells.

"I don't know that you need them anymore," Daniella said. "I mean, if you want to carry them, they can enhance things if you cast the spell, but I think you both are doing well without them."

Dee and DeAnna looked gratified.

"Well, if we're going to be dealing with zombies for the near future, this can stop them."

"And the master," Zane said.

"And the master," I agreed.

"We need to get back on digging up where Mariah Conners went, too," DeAnna said. "I hate that we've not been able to work on that."

"That makes two of us," I said.

Before the zombies had gotten out of control Dee and DeAnna had been working on figuring out where Mariah Conner, hedge witch with a grudge, might have disappeared to.

I didn't want to think about the fact that she might be in her own grave. Granny didn't seem to think she was someone with a normal life span, and most witches weren't. Magic slowed down your aging. We all looked to be in our late twenties.

If Mariah Conners was dead, we were even more up a creek than we already were.

"Well, let's get him," I gestured toward the zombie, "Settled for the night, and we can get back home and get this ready for Deana."

With the six of us, and the shop not open, Dee and DeAnna went back to the house. Deirdre and I went to gather some more herbs to make a whopper of a batch of our spray, and Daniella and Zane tucked the zombie into bed for the night. Within twenty minutes, we were headed back to Pearl Street. Zane parked out back behind our garage and the four of us trooped up the stairs.

When we walked in, Dee and DeAnna were in the kitchen. They turned as we came in from the garage. Goddess be thanked, they had started dinner, and we all sat down together at the table in what used to be the front room. When Meema had moved the house some years ago, she'd expanded it, and remodeled. Now, instead of a house built in the late 1800s, we had an open, modern house, and one that fit our needs.

I'd thought it would be too large when I came back from Hell and Meema was gone. But with Dee and DeAnna here, and Evil and Beeval, and Doc and Granny whooshing in and out, and with Zane popping in—it felt just right.

I was struck, as I was the night before we took on the demon, how lucky I was with my family. I was unlucky as shit with everything else, but my family kicked some major ass.

"What?" I asked, realizing everyone was staring at me.

"Something's up with Deana. If she doesn't call in the next day or two, I'm going to call her," Dee said.

"You said that before," Deirdre said. "We'll send her the spray tomorrow via express mail. Do you think there's something more? How can you tell?"

Dee shrugged. "I don't know. I've just always been able to know when something was coming in terms of family. I knew you three would be calling before you did when Meema died," she smiled a little. "I didn't know why you'd be calling, but I told Mom that we'd be hearing from the crazy Deadwood aunts soon."

"Did DeAnna rip the phone out of the wall?" Daniella teased.

DeAnna rolled her eyes. "I should have."

"You love us," Deirdre said.

"Someone has to," DeAnna retorted, and we all laughed.

Beeval, our house demon, came in wearing Evil, our house chicken, on his head. "Bacon?" he asked.

Evil clucked softly. I loved seeing these two little weird things together. Evil was a rooster that Meema had decided was dinner one night, and she tried to chop off his head. He got away, head hanging off like a bad purse. After a week or so, Meema gave up and healed him magically. Magic can't fix everything, however. Evil was not all that bright and I didn't remember him as all that bright to begin with. He was sweet, however, and that was what counted.

Beeval was a demon, and he'd helped me escape from Hell when Ashlar the greasy asshole demon had dragged me down there with Meema. Meema hadn't been as lucky. Ashlar had sent her to the River of Souls, and tied me to a board so I could watch the floating river of gross moved slowly overhead. I'd been able to escape, but there was no hope for Meema. The thought made me want to cry.

I stopped myself. She would be proud of us. We hardly fought at all, the three of us. We were helping our next generation of family. Granny and Doc were here and had made up. Beeval and Evil got along—loved each other, in fact.

This was the family Meema always strove to build. She'd be happy that her death had pushed us all to try just a little harder.

But I still wanted her here, damn it. Just to have her see what we'd managed to do, despite all our years of fighting.

All the living Nightingales were in one place. And we were happy about it.

"Of course, we have bacon," I said, going to the

fridge and pulling out a package. As I cooked, Beeval watched, Evil sleeping on his head. Beeval made a soft humming noise.

It was great. All of this—it was great. For the moment, anyway. And given the way things were going, we had to take these moments.

"So where do you think Mariah might be?" I asked without turning around.

DeAnna was bringing plates to the sink. "Mariah left after her daughter died. We found the tiniest obituary notice in the archives of the paper."

"Kids died a lot in those days," I said. "Sadly."

I glanced over to see her nodding. "Yes, Mom mentioned that. She said that people always marveled at the four of you—not only because Meema had you, but that all four of you and Meema lived. She said it didn't help your witchy reputation."

I frowned. "She was right. I still think Granny used magic. Like, she either knew that Meema would never get another chance, or she wanted all four of us to live."

"Both, probably," Deirdre said, carrying more plates.

"I wish she could remember," Dee said from the table.

"I don't," Granny materialized from the wall.

"Your ears burning?" Deirdre asked. "Or were you just eavesdropping?"

"Both," Granny snapped. "I honestly don't remember. I put warding spells around your mother, and healing spells, and I was praying to the Goddess every day. She was bigger than a house. Since I'd never seen a woman have more than one baby, I was worried nearly to death, and that's no exaggeration. I wasn't sure what to do beyond herbals and healing spells and protection spells."

"How did she manage to have four of us?" Daniella asked.

Granny shrugged. "I don't know. We talked about it, and best we can figure, between her praying to the Goddess for more than one baby from Jack Fitzgerald before he died, and me setting spells, and your mom setting her own spells after Jack died, they all hit at once. I really don't know," she finished.

"You're not exactly the most reliable narrator," I said.

"Well, you forget things," Granny shrugged again. "I'm glad it worked, though."

"You might as well stay, Granny," Dee said. "We think we traced Mariah."

"Really?" Granny looked pleased at the change of subject.

I was pretty sure she was tired of being badgered but holy hell. She'd left us a mess, one that we were still trying to clean up. And she didn't have answers, which was decidedly inconvenient. Nor was letting things lie the Nightingale way. I snickered to myself.

Granny drifted toward the table where Dee sat. "What did you find?"

"Let me get the dishes out of the way," Dee got up, but I was at her elbow.

"Here, let me get them. Talk loud so we can all hear and you don't have to repeat yourself." I walked back to the kitchen, turning off the stove and depositing the dishes in the sink. Beeval was hopping back and forth on one foot as I patted the bacon down with paper towels. I gave him a plate piled with bacon strips. Balancing the plate, and moving carefully so as not to disturb Evil, Beeval made his way to the table.

We'd told him that he could and should sit with us. In the last week or so, he'd been making the effort. We had a higher chair for him, because he was too short to reach the table if he sat in a different chair.

I thanked the Goddess that we had curtains on the windows and no neighbors on this side. There was no way to explain this one.

"Is she still alive?" I asked.

Dee made a face. "I can't tell. I pulled up the file I was working on. I know where she went. And she has descendants, although I can't tell if it's like you all and your descendants."

"That would be the smart thing to do," Granny said.

"Well?" Daniella asked. "Where is she?"

"We found an article about an herbalist and spiritual woman moving to Cheyenne, Wyoming in 1877, which seems to be the right time. It only lists her as Mrs. Connors," DeAnna said.

"That sounds right, but we have no way of knowing," Deirdre said.

Dee sighed. "We're going to need to go and visit."

"And say what?" I asked. "That your granny cursed ours, and could you manage that?" I smiled at Dee to let her know I wasn't mocking her. "You three were raised with the idea of the crazy Deadwood aunts and some of what goes with that. Most people aren't."

"It's worth a shot," DeAnna said.

"It is," Daniella said slowly. "Someone with that much anger isn't going to let it die with them, if she did in fact die."

"Why wouldn't she?" Dee asked.

"Because witches live longer," Deirdre said.

"Well, then let's plan on that," DeAnna said, as though it were settled. "We traced enough obituaries to know that there are people in her family still there. We can say we're tracking down some of the original people in Deadwood."

"You're becoming quite the sneaky one," I said to DeAnna.

"It's the bad influence of the crazy Deadwood aunts," she replied without cracking a smile.

We talked late into the night, planning for Dee and DeAnna to go to see the Connors, if they were the Connors we were looking for. I had a feeling they were —but I left that out. Dee was already nervous. I could tell that that she was worried for Deana.

I had to wonder what the hell my niece was getting

into. I sent a prayer to the Goddess to keep her safe. Vampires were tricky bastards, and could be extremely ruthless. We mixed a huge batch of the spray, and bottled up five travel sized bottles for Deana.

On Dee's suggestion, we added some vanilla, so it would smell like, with the lavender and vanilla, a body spray. Nothing more. The bottles were carefully packed and Deirdre printed off a tracking slip for the box. It would be picked up first thing in the morning.

Then we bottled a small spray bottle for each of the six of us.

"I think this might take away some of my cool guy points," Zane said.

"I think you're able to handle it," I said, my whole body warming as our eyes met. After a moment, I looked away. "I think we need to go to Deadwood Gulch tomorrow."

"It's Tuesday," Daniella said. "We don't have to open."

"Pretty convenient," Deirdre agreed. "Might as well."

"We can see if we can blast through the spell," I said. I hated the idea that a spell cast by someone else had stopped me. And I made fun of the vampires for having too much pride. "We also need to call Deana and let her know the vampire no more spray is on the way."

There was a moment of silence, and then everyone started to laugh.

"What?" I asked.

"Vampire no more?" Dee asked between laughing.

"Vamp no mo," I said, grinning. "The future of the Nightingale fortune."

I didn't know why, but the name stuck, and by the time we'd cleaned up, VampNoMo was the only thing anyone was calling it.

"If we do sell this, we just call it No More, or Delay Spray," Daniella said. "We'll sell more that way."

"Oooh, I like that. Delay Spray," I said. "But it will always be VampNoMo to me."

She laughed.

We all went upstairs for a last cup of tea, and then everyone went to bed. Leaving me alone with Zane.

Totally not deliberately, I'm sure.

He came to me, and put his arms around me. I let myself relax into him, liking the feeling of having someone I could hug and kiss be a part of my team.

"We still have a date planned," Zane murmured into my hair. "Two more days."

"Yes, we do," I said.

He kissed me, and how long we stood there kissing like teenagers, I wasn't sure. But we stepped back from one another, as though by unspoken agreement. We were taking it slow, and I liked that.

"I'll see you tomorrow."

"Don't go running off to catch zombies by yourself," I teased.

"I'll call you first," he promised. "But otherwise, we're going into the gulch and finish this."

"Abso-fuckin'-lutely," I said.

Zane leaned down to give me one last kiss, and then was out the door.

For the second time in a week, I floated upstairs and went to bed with a smile on my face. It was nice. I could get used to this.

CHAPTER ELEVEN

The next morning, we left Dee and DeAnna at Pearl Street. I reminded them that the delivery guy would be there to pick up the spray for Deana. Daniella, Deirdre, and I headed to the shop. We needed to feed Mr. Shuffles the zombie, and I had to figure out our next move in regards to the person or people hanging out in Deadwood Gulch.

"What is this, a full moon? Is Mercury in retrograde?" I grumbled to no one in particular at the shop as I pulled chicken out of the fridge. "When was the last time we had a month like this?"

"We were due for it," Deirdre said as she pulled out several bags of herbs. We were going to make a few more spell bags, since Dee and DeAnna were coming with us to the gulch, and despite our words of encouragement, they wanted a little boost. We'd need to break them of that, but maybe right now wasn't the best time.

We not only sold loose tea, we sold some loose herbs, for cooking and for what people thought of as spell work. There was a local group of women who bought herbs from us for just that. It was harmless, however. To my way of thinking, better they get it, along with advice, from us than someone else.

Besides, none of them had the talent. I always checked out our local witches, to see if there was anyone we needed to bring into the fold. It hadn't happened in years.

Zane came in through the back door a little later, and I ignored the fact that my heart leapt when I saw him, as well as the fact that he looked really good. "Hey," I said. Focus, I thought.

"Is our friend still here?" he asked, nodding his head in the direction of the basement.

"He is."

"You get the note?"

"Didn't I tell you about it? I did," I said. "I thought I told you about it."

"What did it say? I don't remember you saying anything," Zane asked.

"Daniella, where's the note?"

"On my work tray," Daniella said without looking up from where she was measuring herbs.

I went to find the tray she'd been working on. The note was still there, and I set the tray on the counter in front of us.

Zane put his hands behind his back and leaned

down to inspect the note. "Smells like Note guy," he said.

"Well, I only got it off him recently. It's been with him for quite a while."

"Any idea what the numbers are?" he asked, leaning to one side and then the other looking at the note.

"We don't know. A spell, maybe?"

"Who uses numbers for spells?" Zane asked.

"That was my point," Daniella called out.

I shrugged. "Everyone has their own thing when it comes to spells," I said.

"It's strange," Zane said.

"It is. Note guy gave it up after I got that. The pin holding it on him was spelled—" I stopped as Zane stood up.

"What kind of spell?"

"It hurt when I pulled the pin out. It should be there with the note. I could feel magic on the note, too."

"I wonder who the magic was for," Zane said, looking down at the note again. He pulled out his phone and took a picture of it.

"What do you mean?" I asked.

"Was it for you, or someone who would touch the note, so they didn't touch it? Or was it for the zombie?"

"Why not both?" Deirdre came over, tying off a spell bag. "Here, tie these," she handed me several. "A protection spell and I don't know, an instruction spell all rolled into one?"

"That takes away from both," I said.

"Not if you don't need a lot of juice," Daniella said.

"It seems lazy," I replied.

"It is," Deirdre said. "Totally lazy. Not everyone has our work ethic," she grinned at me. "You think we have enough to make them feel better?"

I nodded. "Let's feed Shuffles," I wondered if it was a bad sign on some front that we kept naming our zombies, "and get back to the house. Once the spray is picked up, we can get going."

I walked down the stairs to the basement, Zane right behind me. I liked that he came with me. Not that there was any reason he needed to. I just liked it.

The zombie was still there—although where would he go?—but he was not as lively. Yesterday, he'd been bumping against the bars of the cage. Now, he was still bumping, but it was slower, less forceful.

Tossing the chicken through the bars, I watched him. It took a moment for the smell of the chicken to hit the zombie. When it did, I could see indecision on him.

"Weird," I muttered, stepping back to watch.

The zombie really wanted the chicken. But he was reluctant to leave off trying to get out. That meant that whatever was driving him was very strong. That didn't seem like the work of a lazy spell caster.

All of the things we were discovering didn't really make sense. It would, though. Once we found the ass who was behind all this. Other people's motives often looked confusing to an outsider.

The chicken finally won, and the zombie fell to the floor, eating enthusiastically.

"One thing taken care of," I said. "Let's get back to Pearl Street."

As we went back upstairs, Zane touched my hand, and with my sisters, we locked up the shop. I felt like one of the reasons we'd survived so long was that we never forgot that we had to live here, had to keep things going, no matter what it was we were fighting against. We always took care of the shop. Even now, when there was a less than welcome visitor there. We always made sure we could still live there after whatever our latest crisis had passed.

That was both the blessing and curse of only having one place you could go. You had to take care of that one place.

Pulling up to the garage at Pearl Street, I saw that the delivery truck was leaving, turning off Pearl Street.

"Did they take the package?" I called out as we all came into the kitchen.

"They did," Dee said. "And gave us a tracking number. It will be there tomorrow."

"Let's call Deana," DeAnna said, watching her daughter.

Deana answered on the first ring, and she sounded tired.

"Put it on speaker," I said.

Dee did so. "We've sent the vamp spray," she said to Deana.

"Call it by its rightful name!" Deirdre shouted.

Dee sighed. "All right, all right. Keep your hair on. The Vamp NoMo spray should be there today."

Deana burst out laughing on the other end of the phone. "Who named that? Gran?" she asked, and we could hear her giggling a little.

That, more than anything, gave me a little hope. Even more than laughter. And I found that I was snickering a little myself at the thought of DeAnna naming it.

"You actually made it!" Deana finished, although I could tell she was trying not to laugh.

"We did, And no, Gran did not name it," Dee said. "As I'm sure you know. It was Daniella. We shipped it express, and it should be there shortly, according to the tracking number."

"What does it do?" Deana asked.

"Spray it at the vampire in question, and they'll fall down in a deep sleep, giving you about seven and a half minutes to get away," Dee smiled as she relayed the results of our experiments.

"What, you tested it?" Deana asked.

"Sort of," Dee hedged.

"What does that mean? This is my ass, Mom."

"Well, there's a zombie in the basement at the shop," Dee said quickly.

I understood her hesitation. It sounded really bad to tell someone we had a zombie in a cage in our tea shop.

"What? Why do you—you know what? Never mind.

I don't want to know right now. But I will be asking for details later. So when you sprayed the zombie, it knocked them for seven plus minutes?" Deana was all business now.

"Yes. On average. Sometimes, it went a little longer. But I think if you plan for six minutes, you'll be fine." Dee looked at us to make sure she had the numbers right.

Deirdre and I nodded at her.

"I love you, Mom," Deana said. I could hear the relief in her tone. "I have until tomorrow. So if things go to shit, I'm out of here. I'll lock up the house."

"Just send me a text. Tell me that you burned a pan, or something," Dee was worried again.

"Mom, thanks. I know you have other things to do," Deana said.

"Well, none of us are on a deadline, so this was more important. How are things on your end?" Dee asked.

I rolled my eyes. Not on a deadline? Please. We lived on deadlines. Then I realized Dee was toning it down so that Deana wouldn't worry. Deana was on her own.

It wasn't very often that I wished we could travel and keep our power. I wanted to be there to help her.

"Not as good as yours. The Vamp NoMo spray is timely," Deana replied. The worry was back.

"Deana, honey, if it comes to that, you run your ass off. You get far away, and don't even text me. But I would appreciate it if you locked down everything whenever you leave the house." Dee's voice was firm.

"I'm doing it now. I need to go into the office, Mom, so I'm going to go," Deana said.

"I wish I was there," Dee said.

"I'm glad you're not," Deana sounded very firm on this. "It would make me worry more. No one's going to come at you up there."

"That's not necessarily a comfort," Dee's brow was wrinkled.

"Nothing is right now. Except NoMo spray." Deana laughed.

Everyone laughed at that and then all of us, the Nightingales and Hollidays, said, "Love you," at the same time.

Dee hung up, and stood still, her hand still on the phone. I moved toward her, giving her a hug. "Deana's going to be all right."

She sighed. "I hope so. I can tell she's out of sorts."

"Can you do that with everyone?" I asked, interested.

Dee shook her head. "No. It comes and goes."

"Careful. You'll be one of the crazy Deadwood aunts before you know it," Daniella teased.

"I'd say that was the least of my problems," Dee responded. "Besides, everyone thinks I'm one of the aunts," she added.

Which was true. She and DeAnna looked older

than the three of us, and the few times they'd been in the shop with us, we'd introduced them as our aunts.

"She is going to be all right," Deirdre said. "She'll have the spray soon, and we've helped her out by giving her an advantage. Now let's go kick our squatter out of Deadwood Gulch. I'm tired of zombies rolling around."

"That makes two of us," DeAnna said. She patted Dee on the shoulder as she walked by. "What do we need?"

"Any of the spell bags you guys want to bring, and good shoes. There's no real trails in the gulch."

It took about thirty minutes, but finally, we were all ready to go. Deirdre drove Daniella, Dee, and DeAnna in her Jeep and Zane and I took the truck. We drove down the CanAm and parked in a parking lot across the highway from where we'd seen the zombie head into the gulch. The popular trail that ran through Deadwood was on this side, and people were used to seeing hikers move back and forth across the highway. We wouldn't stand out.

Well, not any more than normal.

At the edge of the trees, I looked to my sisters. "Ready?"

"Lead the way," Daniella said.

"I can't wait to see this ward," Deirdre said.

We moved single file, with me in the lead. I wasn't sure how long we'd been walking, because I really didn't want to check my watch and see exactly how long —I was worried I'd missed the damn ward.

Given that it had looked to stretch all the way across the gulch, that would really be bad. But just as I was starting to truly doubt myself, I saw the shimmer against the sun.

"There it is," I said, stopping.

Deirdre and Daniella fanned out beside me, looking up at the shimmer.

"I see what you mean," Daniella said. "It does look like it stretches all the way across."

"It's not as visible as I thought," Deirdre was eying the section in front of us.

"Well, let's test it," Daniella said. She raised her hand and sent out a burst of magic toward the ward.

Like it had with me, the magic hit the ward, and rippled out across the ward. The ward shimmered, but didn't change.

"Can we break it?" Dee moved next to me.

"We have to," Deirdre said.

"It's going to take all of us," Zane said. "This is a strong ward."

"Open the way?" I looked to both my sisters.

Daniella nodded. "That will work." She glanced at Dee, DeAnna and Zane. "We're all going to say *Aperi modo* when I count to three."

"Which means?" Dee asked.

"Open the way," Deirdre said. "It's general enough to cover several different versions of a warding spell. We don't know how this was set, so you want to be general to see if you can hit the right note."

Dee and DeAnna nodded

"All right, ready?" Daniella asked. At the murmur of assent, she said, "One, two, three!"

"*Aperi modo!*" We all shouted together.

There was a moment of silence, and then the ward rippled.

"Again!" Deirdre said.

"*Aperi modo!*" It was louder this time.

There went our stealth mode. I decided I didn't care. Let whoever this was know that we were coming.

The ward rippled again, larger ripples this time. Then, as though it had never been there, the ward vanished.

"Did we do it?" DeAnna whispered.

"I think so," I said, moving forward.

"Looking to get knocked on your ass again?" Deirdre asked, amusement in her words.

"I'm always willing to take one for the team," I grinned. This was where I felt comfortable. Fighting, kicking ass, taking names. It had been too long since we'd done any of that.

We moved forward, the three of us in front with Zane, Dee, and DeAnna in the back. I let my magic flow through me, loving how it felt on my fingertips, ready to go at a moment's notice.

There wasn't really a path, but I could tell that someone—or something—had been walking through here, because there was a slightly worn trail in front of us.

"The numbers!" Zane exclaimed behind me.

"What?" We all stopped to look at Zane.

"The numbers, on the note. I think I know what they are."

"Is now really the time for this?" I asked.

"Give me one minute, because I think now is definitely the time for this," Zane said. He pulled out his phone, typing quickly.

"What is it?" Daniella asked, sounding frustrated. Which was saying something, because she was the easygoing one of the three of us.

"The numbers may be coordinates," Zane said, a note of triumph in his voice. "Look. When you line them up, they make sense." He showed me his phone.

"What kind of coordinates?" I asked, peering down at the screen.

"Latitude and longitude," Zane replied. "I put them in the map, and what do you know? They point to a spot further down this very gulch, along the hillside," he pointed to the left. "Right over there."

"Maybe we'll keep you," DeAnna said. "Good thinking, Zane."

"Well, I don't know that they are actually coordinates, but it beats just wandering around in here," Zane said.

"Then lead the way," I moved aside.

Holding out his phone, Zane strode ahead of us.

"Be ready," I said to Deirdre and Daniella. "Get your spell bags," I looked over my shoulder at Dee and

Deirdre. "If the boogeyman jumps out, we need to blast him back to whatever rat hole he came out of."

Zane began walking off toward the left at an angle, following the map on his phone.

We started to move up the hill. After about fifteen minutes, Zane stopped.

I nearly bumped into him. "Why'd you stop?"

"I think I found our zombie maker," he said as he pointed up the hill.

There was a note I couldn't identify in his voice.

I stepped around him, and looked to where he was pointing.

It was a small cave opening.

"The cave?" I asked.

"Can't you feel it?" Zane asked.

"I can," Dee said. "What is it?"

"That is a hell of a lot of magic. It's not good to have this much magic in one place," I said. I had a bad feeling about this, in every way that you could have a bad feeling.

"I didn't even know this was here," Daniella said.

"When was the last time we had a reason to be down here?" I shrugged. There were a lot of things to beat yourself up over when you were thinking about what you might have missed in a situation, but this wasn't one of them.

"That's true. But did you know there was a cave?" Deirdre asked.

"Nope. Now we do." I flexed my shoulders, swinging

my arms back and forth. "Let's go say hello." I stepped in front of Zane, the magic visibly coiling around my hands. I was done with this bullshit.

Even though I didn't know for sure this was the guy, or that it was a guy, or that this was the place—this was the guy, and this was the place. Bad feelings and all.

"Wait for us, crazy Deadwood aunt," Deirdre muttered. She and Daniella were beside me in a moment. Together, we walked up the hill.

If I were a magic user hiding in this cave, and I saw us coming, I'd be shitting my pants. I could feel the magic all around the three of us. Even with all the magic he was hoarding up in that cave. Like a shitty dragon, I thought.

Then I felt a jolt, and I glanced over my shoulder to see that Dee and DeAnna had joined us. Crazy Deadwood aunts, indeed.

Zane came to stand next to Daniella.

"Let's go," I said.

We made it up the hill, and at the mouth of the cave, Zane held up his hand, allowing a light to spring up from his palm. He held his hand high.

The cave was dark, and smelled moldy.

"There's nothing here," Dee said.

"Wait," I said.

I could smell something else, something that smelled like magic, and burnt feathers. "*Ostende!*" I shouted, my words echoing around the entrance.

Nothing for a moment, and then the wall shimmered. The cave stretched back, and in the distance, I could see a light.

"This is an old mine shaft," Deirdre said. "Clever."

"Why dig something out when you could just use what's there?" Zane asked.

"I don't like this at all," DeAnna said.

"I'm with you," I replied. "This sucks. But we're going to do it anyway, and clean house of whatever the filth is that's camped out here."

I walked ahead, magic at the ready. Something moved in front of me and I sent a fire spell shooting toward it.

The light from the fire showed that I'd blasted a zombie. It stared at me dully, unaware that its sleeve was on fire.

"Oh, for Goddess' sake," Daniella said. She sent a blast of water toward it, and the cave was darker again as the zombie went out.

"Stand still," I said quietly.

Nothing moved. Not even the zombie.

"Why isn't he moving?" Deirdre whispered.

Zane turned on the flashlight on his phone, and we all peered at the zombie. It didn't move, didn't look like it had moved since Daniella put out the fire.

"What's going on with him?" DeAnna asked, leaning over my shoulder.

"I don't know," I said. "But I sure don't like it." Now I knew we were dealing with a necromancer. Mages used what could be termed as dark magic, but not like this.

They preferred more spell work, like witches. Necromancers, on the other hand, seemed to view zombies like pets. Disposable pets, which was even worse.

"Let's keep going," Zane said, easing out in front of me. He held up his phone, the flashlight shining in front of him. "We're almost to the end."

"Hang on," I said. I sent a spell to the zombie, and there was a puff as the spell hit him. The body crumpled. I knew that the head had fallen to the side, but there was no need to mention that.

I just didn't want whomever we found in here to have this one more zombie at their disposal.

I wished I could tell everyone to walk a little more quietly. We sounded like a herd of elephants. But finally, we made it back to where we'd seen light flickering.

The cave opened up into a semi-round room. I couldn't see any more tunnels branching off from the room, which meant that this had started life as a mine, and been abandoned.

There were lanterns around the room, and along the left side, lying in rows, were zombies. There had to be at least ten of them. I peered at them. They seemed to be in some sort of stasis.

Why?

And there was a man. Dressed in jeans and a plaid shirt, he had his back to us. He was tall, but not too tall, and had short hair that looked light brown in the light.

"Did you see the sarcophagus?" he asked. His voice

was pleasant, the voice of a man getting his chores done.

When there was no answer, he turned around to look right at us.

"Dad?" Zane's voice was incredulous, full of disbelief.

CHAPTER TWELVE

"What are you doing here?" Zane was appalled. I could see it written all over him.

But he wasn't completely surprised.

The man in front of us laughed. Had it been something I'd seen on TV, I would have changed the channel for the overreacting. Jesus. This dude needed to get out more. I looked him over, and revised my opinion. I could smell the grave dirt from here, and he stunk.

Maybe he needed to stay here.

Well, maybe not here.

"Good to see you finally figured it out, boy," the man said. "Took you long enough, didn't it? You always were slow."

"What do you want?" Zane asked, his tone calm again.

"Who are your friends, Zane? Introduce me,

please." The man came forward, wiping his hands on his pants.

While he stank, and we were in a cave with snoozing zombies, this man had courtly manners.

Big ass phony.

"These are the Nightingales," Zane said.

"I thought there were only three of them," his dad said, looking around Zane at the five of us.

"Surprise," I said. My voice came out harsh, and I didn't care. Mostly because I was wondering what we were going to do with this guy. And whether or not Zane knew this was his dad. His dad!

The man continued to eye us like we were livestock. "They look like fine ladies," he said, smiling. Like we weren't standing right here in front of his bananapants self. "My son never was one for manners. I am delighted to meet you at last, for your reputation proceeds you." He inclined his head. "I am Brian Earl DeGroat."

"DeGroat?" I looked at Zane.

"When my father threw me out, I changed my name. Why are you here?" Zane ground out.

"Threw you out? That's certainly an exaggeration." DeGroat looked at Zane like he'd caught him with his hand in the cookie jar. "Really."

"What would you call telling your son to get out of your sight and don't come back?" Zane asked, his voice flat.

"A measure of the intensity of the situation," DeGroat said.

"The one with Zane's mother?" I asked. I could feel Deirdre and Daniella look at me, and I realized I hadn't shared this with them. Shit. It wasn't like there had been a lot of time. Additionally, I didn't feel it was my story to tell.

Brian Earl DeGroat let down his mask of pleasantry. "You told her about that, Zane? That time when you killed your mother?"

I heard the gasps behind me. I didn't turn around. "I'm sure you forgot it was that time when he put her zombie to rest," I smiled sweetly.

DeGroat narrowed his eyes at me, and then turned his attention back to Zane. "What am I doing here? Well, it's all due to you, Zane," the man said. "For which I thank you."

What? What the fuck? I turned to look at Zane. His father saw me, and started to laugh. Again with the overacting. I had a feeling, however, this was how the guy was all the time.

"I want Deadwood," DeGroat said, all the laughter gone now.

"What are you doing with the zombies?" Daniella asked.

"Why here?" Zane asked, his hand reaching out to touch my arm.

Like he knew what I was thinking.

I'd been ready to blast the shit out of dear old Dad, but stilled myself at Zane's question.

DeGroat shrugged. "The ley lines are strong here.

They allow me to keep my friends, even those who are a little older, in usable condition."

"What are you doing with the zombies?" Daniella asked again. DeGroat couldn't hear it, but Daniella was fast losing her patience with him.

Not to mention that statement, that right there—that's why I hated necromancers. Such arrogant assholes. Also, Brian Earl DeGroat was lying like a rug right now. We could add liar to his personality traits.

"You can't have Deadwood," Zane said.

"Says who? You and the wand waver?" DeGroat asked, his lips turning up in a sneer. "As for my friends, they help me with what I am seeking. These—" he gestured to the zombies on the floor—"Are resting, gathering their strength."

"I don't use a wand," I informed him. "That's for amateurs. And we need to talk about your abuse of these people." I waved my hand toward the zombies that were lying on the floor. Gathering their strength? He was having them do something that was draining them. Interesting.

If we took out DeGroat, I'd bet we'd have no more zombie issues.

DeGroat cackled again. "Whatever. Be quiet, witch. Let your betters speak, even if my son is a complete disappointment."

I took a step forward, the magic coiling in my fingers. Zane stuck out his arm, stopping me. "No," he said quietly.

"Your son just saved your sorry ass," I told DeGroat. "You should be grateful." I felt my sisters move closer to me, ready for whatever was coming.

"You don't have anything to say about this," DeGroat said.

"Actually," I stepped around Zane's arm. "I do. This is my town and you are not welcome."

DeGroat stared at me for a moment, then laughed. It was a full-bodied laugh, booming and amused. "Your town? A hedge witch? Really?" He laughed again. "I'd heard about the Nightingales, but I've been doing whatever I wanted since I showed up. And this is the first time I've seen you. So I think perhaps it's not really your town, but there for the taking."

I could feel the magic tingling in my fingers, ready to come out and play. This asshole was just the kind of guy I liked to blast into last week. And I was never sure why they always wanted to call us hedge witches. Given the one *we* were looking for, and not finding, I'd say they were pretty damn powerful. And given our history —we weren't exactly unskilled.

But that was necromancers. Thank Goddess that Zane wasn't like dear old dad. He would have been dead and buried by now.

"Yes, really. I'm Desdemona Nightingale, and along with my sisters Deirdre, Daniella, Dee, and DeAnna, I don't put up with the kind of nonsense you bring," I gestured at him in a dismissive manner, guaranteed to piss him off. I also found that there was power in names.

I was good like that. I had to work to keep the smile off my face. "It's not welcome here in Deadwood. And we certainly don't condone the robbing of our graves," I pasted a bright smile on my face. "Or putting the departed to work. None of that goes here. So you'll need to run along," I made the gesture again.

I was spoiling for a fight, and this joker seemed just the type to give it to me.

"Des," Zane said low, so low that I almost didn't hear him.

I ignored him.

Zane turned to his father. "Dad, you need to leave. Like, leave town. This isn't a place for you."

The man stared at Zane as though he'd never seen him before. "It's hard to believe I raised you," he said conversationally, as though this wasn't about to be the OK Corral in about three seconds flat.

"I find that hard to believe myself," I chimed in. "Zane's polite, and professional, and not an asshole."

The man's brows drew together, and I could feel magic around him. Certain magic has a smell, almost like ozone. He was obviously itching for a fight as well. But something in his son's face stopped him.

I saw it—it was something, and I was dying to turn and look at Zane, but I didn't take my eyes off his dad.

"I will take my leave," Brian Earl DeGroate said formally. "For the time being. But I want Deadwood,

Zane, and I will have it. Along with everything else I seek." With a scornful glance at me, he whirled away.

If he'd had a cape, it would have been right out of a Vegas show, he was so dramatic.

As we watched, he shimmered, and disappeared.

"Wow," I said. "So that was your dad."

Zane sighed, the sound of a much older, tired man. "Yes."

"What does he want with Deadwood?"

"He wants it because I'm here."

"Seriously?" I did look at Zane then. "That's it?"

Zane nodded. "He's every single bad stereotype rolled into one angry ball."

"I don't think that's it," Deirdre said.

"Yeah, he gave in way too easily, especially after insulting you in every way he could," Daniella said. "There's something more to this. He doesn't really give a shit about you, or us. Outside of how we might screw up his plans."

Zane looked at her, and I could see warring emotions on his face. He wanted to believe this wasn't personal. He really, really wanted to believe.

I sighed. "Great. So he's going to hang around? You think this is his whole stash of the undead?" I pointed at the poor zombies still on the floor. They hadn't moved during any of this.

"That was a pretty good piece of magic," Deirdre said. "The whole swirly, whoosh, and gone thing."

"It's one of his specialties," Zane said.

"Did you know it was him?" I asked, remembering the lack of surprise when his dad turned around.

"No, but when I saw him, I wasn't surprised at all. Because of course who else would it be?" Zane's voice was bitter.

"Well, standing around here isn't going to solve a thing," DeAnna said. "Why don't we help the zombies along to a final resting place, and go home?"

I didn't like it. I didn't like that Brian Earl DeGroat was still walking around, agenda in hand, planning on doing things in my town. I didn't like it at all. But DeAnna was right. We needed to get these zombies free of whatever it was DeGroat had been doing with them, and get the hell out of here.

When we went to move the zombies, several of them started to fall apart.

"Oh, for Goddess' sake," Deirdre said. "We'll need to levitate them."

We avoided obvious magic like this. But here in a gulch that was relatively deserted, I thought we might be able get away with it.

"Can you all glom on here?" I asked Dee. "I know we haven't taught you this yet, but just sending helping thoughts."

"Lifting thoughts," Daniella said.

"We can do that," DeAnna said.

Carefully, we maneuvered all ten of the zombies out of the mine. When we came to the opening, I stopped. "Hang on. Let me look around. We need to dig a spot for them, and I want to make sure that no one is around."

"No one comes down here," Daniella said.

"Yeah, but it will be just our luck that a hiker was feeling frisky today, or something equally random," I said.

"She's right," Deirdre said. "That's the only sort of luck we seem to have."

I walked out, looking for a good spot. A bit north of the cave was open ground, and I used magic to dig out a place where we could bury them. When I walked back to the cave, everyone was shifty and impatient.

"I thought you went home or something," DeAnna snarked.

"I already have their grave. All we need to do is get them in and end it."

"Oh," DeAnna said. "Well, that's good then."

I smiled in the darkened entrance. I didn't mind that she was getting snarky. I kind of liked it. Sass was always better than accepting shit.

We floated the poor things out of the mine, and over to the grave, letting them come to rest gently in the dirt.

"What now?" asked Dee.

"You might want to look away," I said.

Dee shook her head. "No. We're all in this together."

"All right," I said. "Deirdre? Daniella?"

They knew what to do. We'd done this far too many times before. We clasped hands, and together, we said, "Separatum finis vitae."

There was a muffled blast of dirt around the zombies, and their heads rolled slightly, no longer attached to their bodies.

"Whoa," said DeAnna. "Holy hell. That was..."

"It's not something we like doing, but it gets things done quickly, and without dragging things out for them," I said. The sight of so many people, pulled from the grave and used by that stinky peacock of a man... it made my blood boil.

We moved the dirt over them.

"Could he come back and bring them back?" Dee asked.

"No. By separating the head from the body, it makes them useless as a zombie," Daniella said.

"Well, good." DeAnna said. "They deserve peace."

"They always do," Deirdre said. "We need to get back to Pearl Street. We have work to do. Research," she nodded, and turned away.

I recognized her stride. It was her pissed off walk. Brian Earl DeGroat didn't know what was coming to me.

"Research what?" Daniella asked, hurrying to catch up to Deirdre.

We all were. She was fast when she got into her huffy walk.

"Didn't you hear him when we first came in?" Deirdre called over her shoulder. "It doesn't matter. I heard enough. Come on."

We were out of the woods and the gulch in record

time, and before I knew it, on our way to Pearl Street. I rode back with Zane.

"You all right?" I asked.

He shook his head. "I don't know what I am. I haven't seen him since the night I left. You know I didn't bring him here, don't you?" He turned to look at me.

I nodded slowly. "But you weren't surprised."

"Because this is so him. Just move in, toss zombies around, and go after whatever it is he wants."

I was thinking about what Deirdre had said. "The sarcophagus!" I exclaimed.

"What?"

"I'll bet that's what Deirdre is talking about. Hurry, let's get back." I didn't want to talk. I wanted to start researching, and not think about how unsettled I felt about this in regards to Zane. To cover my messy feelings, I asked, "Do you think he brought all those zombies here?"

Zane shook his head. "I don't know. They don't have the... um... flavor of my dad."

I stared. "Ew. Just ew, Zane. What does that even mean?"

He shrugged, looking embarrassed. "Every necromancer has their own style, like every witch. I saw enough of the zombies my dad created to know he didn't make these."

"Everyone has their own flavor?" I held up a hand. "You have to stop there. I'm stuck on that part."

"I know, it's gross. I can't help that I'm related to the guy. But you can see why I left."

"Well, yeah. But what really made you leave? Was there more than your mom?" I hadn't asked him this since he told me about his mom. I mean, who would, right? But the way his dad talked—not that his dad was to be trusted—I needed to find out more, not directly in this manner, with no room for wiggling away, or changing the subject.

Zane looked more uncomfortable than I'd ever seen him, and that made all my red flags go right up the mast and fly at full speed. "He wanted us to work together. Most of us can't. We're solitary."

"Because you're all egomaniacs," I interjected. "Well, you're not. But you know what I mean."

"Sharing much of anything isn't a strong point," Zane agreed. "It's different with your kid, I guess. I told him no, I wanted to study more, and there were different things I was interested in. This was before I walked in on him with my mom's zombie."

"Such as?" I asked.

"Well, I'm not really fond of zombies. Not getting them, or animating them, or anything. My dad likes to use them for..." he stopped, looking embarrassed again.

"For?" I prompted.

"As a method of persuasion. Do what you're asked, or zombies will start hanging around your home, or your business." He looked out the window, his expression bleak

I threw up my hands. "Of course he did. No matter that they're people! Who had loved ones! Who—"

Zane held up a hand. "I know. I know! You don't have to tell me, Desdemona!"

I stopped. I could tell that he was upset, and I didn't want to make it worse. I knew he was upset about his mom, and having to put zombies that his dad had in service probably stirred up a lot of shit. But—"You know he can't stay here," I warned.

"I know. I don't know how to make him leave, though. The more we push, the more he'll dig his heels in," Zane looked miserable. "Tonight was too easy. Deirdre's right."

"Zane, you know we protect Deadwood," I said.

"I know, no exceptions," Zane finished.

I'd never seen him look so miserable, and I felt... bad... that I'd had to make him feel this way.

I scooted over the seat in the truck, and threaded my arm through his. Touching him sent an electric jolt down my arm from my hand.

"Desdemona," he whispered. We were stopped at a stoplight, and as though he couldn't help it, his head bent to mine, and I let my eyes close. I knew it wasn't smart, wasn't the best choice, blah blah blah. I didn't care.

Zane's lips touched mine, and I felt myself nearly go up in flames. His lips were soft, and firmly pressed against mine when—

A horn honked behind us, making both of us laugh

a little. Zane hit the gas, and we moved forward. I leaned my head on his shoulder, liking the way he felt next to me.

After a moment, he pulled over onto the shoulder, and buried his face in my neck. I could feel his anger, and shame, and sadness. No one likes to discover their parent is an even bigger jerk than they thought.

Although we'd found out Granny had left us with some serious shit, and we just got mad. Well, if Zane hung around long enough, maybe he'd get some of that mad reaction thing. Please, please, please don't let this be a farce, I thought. Please let this be real.

I don't know how long we sat on the side of the road, but eventually, he moved away from me, and got back onto the highway. We didn't talk as he drove through downtown Deadwood. When he pulled the truck into Pearl Street, I slid back across the seat, and walked through the open garage door. Coming into the kitchen, I saw that my sisters and nieces were already at the table, peering at their laptops.

"OK, what did I miss?" I asked. For today being kind of a bust, I was feeling pretty good. And I was fairly certain it had everything to do with Zane.

Which was... disconcerting.

Please let this be real.

"When we came in, DeGroat—and where did you get the last name McCallister, anyway?" Deirdre asked.

"It was my mother's maiden name," Zane replied, his face stony.

"Well, I can see why you and your dad don't pal around," Daniella said.

"When we came in," Deana began again, "He asked, 'Did you see the sarcophagus?' like it was something that whoever he was expecting knew all about."

"OK," I said.

"And he said something about ley lines, which, while it was kind of bullshit, wasn't total bullshit."

"You know this how?" I asked.

Deirdre pushed her hand through her hair. "So I went onto the message boards."

Deirdre loved the message boards. Normally, they came through for her. Although her search for Mariah Connors hadn't gotten any bites, she had a pretty good rate of success.

"I'd just seen a thread about ley lines, and I went back through it. There are ley lines here."

"There are ley lines everywhere," I said.

"Yes, but our ley lines, the ones here in Deadwood, they're special. Like everything else around this joint, there's something different about them," Deirdre said.

"And that is? Spit it out," Daniella said. "You're enjoying this way too much."

I sat down on the end of the bench. Zane didn't sit down, choosing to walk to the window and stare out. Moody Zane was back. Well, he'd have to take care of himself for the time being.

Doc and Granny drifted down the spiral staircase, obviously interested in our conversation. All the better.

It would mean we wouldn't need to repeat this fourteen times.

"Our ley lines are like rainbows—there's a pot of gold at the end of them. Well, not gold. This is Deadwood. There's a sarcophagus."

"What the hell are you talking about?" I asked.

Deirdre sighed loudly. "OK, once more for you slow folk," she glared right at me. "Our ley lines have a secret. A treasure, if you will."

"How is it we didn't know about this?" I glared right back. It was our business to know about Deadwood.

"When have we ever had to do diddly with ley lines?" Daniella asked. "We've always had enough to do on a daily basis."

That was fair, but I was tired of finding out shit after the fact. "What's the treasure?"

"It's a sarcophagus," Deirdre said, rolling her eyes.

"What's so special about it?" I asked.

"It's not what's special about the sarcophagus itself—"

"I think you just like saying the word," DeAnna said.

Deirdre continued, "But what's in it. There's a djinn inside."

"It's a genie in a coffin?" I asked. I fought back the urge to laugh. I knew it was because this day had already gone sideways, but the words brought a visual to mind, and it was hard to turn that visual off.

Deirdre nodded. "This is not proven, or anything else. And it's not a new thread, but this is the story. A couple of hundred years ago, some demon got a wild hair after getting hold of a djinn, and locked him up in the sarcophagus. There are a lot of urban legends about what the demon did to the djinn, that they were a couple, that the djinn wanted to be a demon, all sorts of stupid stuff like that." She pointed at the screen of her laptop. "But all of them point to a demon grabbing a djinn, doing something to the djinn, and stuffing him in a coffin."

"Why is it always demons?" I asked the room in general.

"Because they live to annoy," Daniella said.

"You think that's what my dad is after?"

"Is there any other reason he'd be after an old coffin?" Dee asked. Her voice was kind, as if she could tell this was tough on Zane.

"I haven't seen him in almost fifteen years. I have no idea what he'd do—but he doesn't have boundaries." Zane kept his post at the window.

"Have you checked the ley lines?" I asked Deirdre.

"Of course. I'm looking at them right now. And I know why DeGroat hasn't found it yet, if it's even there."

"Why?"

"The standard maps have the ley lines crossing slightly off from where they are, according to all the ley lines people," Deirdre gestured at her laptop again. "For whatever reason, whoever made the map here wasn't as exact as they should have been."

"Maybe that was deliberate," Dee said.

"What do you mean?" Daniella asked.

"Well, if there was a treasure, and the ley lines marked where the treasure, whatever it was," Dee gestured vaguely in the air, "I wouldn't draw a straight line to it."

"Dee, you're brilliant," I said, smiling.

"I know that. About time you all figured it out," Dee said.

"We don't even know that there's a treasure, much less if it's still there," Zane said.

"But the off-center ley lines are a good clue," Deirdre said. "If I had a treasure—and can you imagine demon infused djinn power? Holy shit—I'd hide it too, and only tell my descendants about it."

"Or the entire internet," Daniella said.

"Oh, well, you know you can't keep anything completely secret. One of the descendants or someone in love with the demon or whatever found out, and ran their mouth. No one's picked up on the fact the lines might be off on purpose."

"OK, so if they're not right on purpose, you have to figure out which way they've been moved, and how far. I think you might be looking for the Loch Ness monster," I said.

When Deirdre glared, I spread my hands out in front of me in defense. "What? I'm not trying to be a killjoy, but that's realistic. And now we're on the clock. We have to get to this thing before DeGroat does."

"He's following the known map. That zombie you

found at the old mine site, Zane? That's where the ley lines intersect." Daniella didn't look up from her laptop.

"So what are you saying?" I asked.

"Looks like we're going to be doing some digging."

---

*W*e spent the next day digging in spots that Deirdre picked off the map. I also went to the claim where Zane had picked up one of the zombies. There had to be a reason DeGroat had him digging there. At the end of the first day, I came back to Pearl Street, hot, tired, and grumpy.

"That was a bust," I said. "Not to mention, I had to sweet talk Gunilla and Larson Beck."

"Why?" Deirdre asked.

"Because the Olaf Seim claim belongs to them. And someone told them we were up there, poking around." I was annoyed we hadn't thought to call them beforehand.

"What did you tell them?" Daniella asked. She'd spent the day at the library, looking around the old maps. You'd think that they'd be lacking in accuracy, but this was mining country, and people surveyed things to the inch, because that inch could be the difference between bust and boom.

"I told them that we were working on some facial masks, and were testing various areas around Deadwood to see what might be a good fit."

"Did they buy it?" Dee asked.

"No. Gunilla told me that while sulfur might not be so bad, pyrite was downright dangerous, and I should seriously rethink my business plan." I still smarted at her dressing me down. I'd had to think fast about why it was we were trespassing.

Because we were.

And then I thought about how it was really fucking unfair that zombies had been up here for who knew how long, including one who'd been digging on their claim, and no one noticed. Let one of us Nightingales head up to the place, however, and it was call for the cavalry.

Yeah, I was still a little testy.

Deirdre laughed. "I can see her telling you that."

"I don't have to pretend to see her," I grumped. "I can still hear her."

"So you're going to need to come up with a better plan."

"You just hate getting caught with your pants down," Daniella said.

"Don't you?" I asked. "We do have to live here. Now I look silly for not knowing they had a pyrite claim."

"Did you tell them you didn't know?" Dee asked.

"No. I said that I'd read it was sulfur in this area, and that's why I was here. Gunilla was happy to enlighten me."

"She didn't mean any harm," Deirdre said. "You know that."

"I know, I know. This is just frustrating."

"We have to find it before DeGroat. Speaking of which," Deirdre's tone changed.

"What?" I asked.

"You think Zane really didn't know his dad was here stirring up shit?"

Everyone turned to look at me.

"I do," I said. "It's not my tale to share, but there is a reason he and his dad are not close."

"Outside of being a creepy necromancer?" DeAnna asked, wrinkling her nose.

"Well, there is that," I said. "I think we have a date tonight."

"You didn't tell us that!" Dee got up. "That's a good thing, Desdemona. Go out with him tonight—"

"Even if he might be the enemy," Deirdre said.

"Shut up," Daniella glared at Deirdre.

"And enjoy yourself," Dee finished. She glared at Deirdre as well.

"I don't know if I should," I said. Zane hadn't said anything, even though this was the third day after our first date, and I hadn't seen much of him today, as he'd been tasked with seeing if he could track down his father.

I'd suggested earlier that Brian Earl DeGroat had gone back to the mine where we found him in Deadwood Gulch, but no one was interested in my opinion, so I'd taken myself off to the mine site where I'd been schooled by Gunilla.

"Yes, you should," DeAnna said. "For the same reason we sent Deana back to Los Angeles. You have to keep living, even as the world is burning down around you."

"I know," I said. "Thank you for reminding me." This was part of why I didn't date. You got all soft, and mushy, and worried about things you didn't normally worry about.

"Go," DeAnna said.

I went up to my room, and showered. I had no idea what we were doing tonight. So I dressed a bit more casually, in black capris and a crop top. I might be over a century old, but I can still rock a crop top without too much shame.

When I came downstairs, everyone's eyes moved up to me.

"Zane came by," Deirdre said.

"Where is he?" I asked, looking around.

"He said he needed to cancel tonight," Daniella said.

I didn't look around. I didn't want to see the pity and whatever the fuck else might be there. I turned, went to my room, and closed the door.

I was done for the day. Just done. But I couldn't quit. Nightingales didn't quit. Even when things completely and utterly sucked.

While part of me felt like I was going full on drama over a canceled date, the other part of me was swirling with red flags. It was like a hurricane warning inside my head. Something was up, and it was up with Zane.

It had to do with his dad. And he hadn't told me. Which was not good.

"Fuck this," I said, looking at my sad face in the mirror. Who was this woman? Not Desdemona Nightingale. "No more romance," I said.

I changed into pajamas and went back downstairs.

Everyone looked up at me again.

"Since you all are looking for where the sarcophagus might be, I'll take the Connors family," I said.

No one asked me anything. No one gave me any grief, pity, sympathy, or anything else.

Which was just the way I liked it.

When I finally went to bed that night, I had narrowed down the four names that I thought might either be Mariah Connors, or be related to her. Which felt good. We had too many balls in the air.

Time to take back control and put all the things that were pulling on me and on us in their proper place and get Deadwood—and our lives—back on the rails again.

Because that kind of balance was what made daily life better. And frankly, it had been too long since we'd had that balance.

CHAPTER THIRTEEN

*W*hen I woke the next morning, the sun was higher than normal in the sky. I looked at the clock and realized I'd slept in a lot later than I normally would. It was after eleven. I got a shower and went downstairs.

To my surprise, my entire family was there. Zane, thankfully, was not. Which I was glad to see. My resolve was steady, but seeing him would make it tough. I hoped he'd stay gone another day or two while I put my internal shit in order.

"What's up?" I asked. I noticed that the mood around the kitchen was rather glum.

"Deana called. She had to leave Los Angeles, and leave our house," DeAnna said.

"Why?" I asked, sitting down at the island.

Deirdre set a cup of tea in front of me. I smiled in thanks.

"Because that dumb ass friend of hers had to have her help, and then the vampires wanted her," DeAnna said furiously.

"There's something more," Dee said. She was quieter than her mom.

"What do you mean?" I asked.

"There's something big she's not telling us. I have no idea what it is, because having to haul ass out of town is pretty big," Dee said. "But it's something."

"Where is she going?" I asked.

"I don't know. I told her I didn't want to know."

"Did she tell you why she left? Who was bothering her?" Maybe it was time to call in a few favors with the vampires, and remind them that they didn't fuck with us.

"Settle down, crazy Deadwood auntie," Daniella said.

"That's never going to die, is it?" DeAnna asked.

"Nope. You're one of them now, too," I said, grinning at her. "You know that, right?"

"It's karma," DeAnna said.

"Or a blessing," Deirdre said.

We all smiled, and I felt better. This was us. Smiles out of a veritable shitstorm. While this one wasn't roaring up on our front lawn, it was still a shitstorm.

"Does Deana know to call?" I asked.

Dee nodded. "She does. And she will."

"All right. We need to trust that she's a big girl, and she knows how to handle herself," I said. "Let's find that damn demon genie and see if we can't track down the origin of our curse. Despite appearances, I don't want to die. Or have anyone I love die." I was going to be cheerful if it killed me.

But strangely, it wasn't killing me. Faking it 'til you made it was making me feel better.

Good.

Fuck all the haters, I thought.

"Maybe we're going about this all wrong," Deirdre said.

"Which what are you talking about?" I asked.

"The ley lines. Maybe we need to activate them."

"And we do that how?" Daniella asked.

"We're witches. We magic. So let's magic," Deirdre said.

I opened my mouth and closed it. She was right. Sometimes the simplest answer was the best.

"OK, what do we need?" I asked.

"Nothing but us, and a shovel," Deirdre said.

We all piled into her Jeep, and headed south. The Olaf Seim mine was south of us, outside of Deadwood proper. That's where the ley lines were supposed to be.

Deirdre pulled over.

"Here?" Daniella asked.

Deirdre nodded.

"We're awfully exposed out here," DeAnna said as we all trooped up the hill.

"You'll get used to it. Everyone thinks we're weirdos.

That's why I got a lecture instead of a ticket yesterday," I said. "It's a good cover."

"That's true. I'm not used to being the weirdo," Dee said.

I didn't say anything, just followed Deirdre up to the top of the hill. We could see the town in the distance, and the road down below us.

"Now what?" I asked.

"Everyone clasp hands," Deirdre said. "I had to make this up on the fly, but I think it will work. The spell is Activate Navitas. When you say it, imagine the lines glowing like fairy lights, like a pathway. Got it?" She looked around.

I nodded.

We all clasped hands, and I closed my eyes. I imagined the ley lines like small, thin gold lines that were all around. I loved the idea of fairy lights.

"Activate Navitas!" Deirdre shouted.

"Activate Navitas!" we all echoed.

There was silence, and I felt a humming, almost from someone next to me. I opened one eye, and I could see thick, greenish gray lines forming around us, pushing up the dirt and ground.

"Deirdre?" I whispered. "I think it's working."

These were nothing like I imagined. They were powerful, pulsing with what felt like a heartbeat. The heartbeat of the Earth. This was wild magic, old magic. It didn't give a shit about us, or anything else.

Most magic had intent, based on who was casting it.

This—this was like nothing I'd ever felt before. It rushed through me like a wave, like what being knocked down by the ocean would feel like. I'd never been to the ocean, but this is what it would feel like.

I was at the mercy of a power that I had no control over, a power that didn't care about me, and to whom I was merely a stone on the road.

Tightening my hands around Daniella and DeAnna's, I closed my eyes again and let it take me. There was no sense in fighting this kind of power.

When I let it have its way, it was like a bird flying high into the sky, freed from a cage. The exhilaration, the feeling of daring to go so high—wow.

I didn't want it to stop.

"I'm here," I murmured.

I heard someone else say something, but I didn't know what it was, and I didn't care. I wanted to keep moving, keep going higher. There was nothing else. Nothing else mattered.

Something grabbed at me, and I shook it off. I could not be stopped—would not be stopped.

Then I yelled as I fell to the ground, Deirdre and Dee on top of me, and my ass hurting where I'd fallen into a sitting position.

"What the hell?" I shouted.

"Des, look at yourself," Deirdre said. "Look at your feet."

The green gray of the ley lines pulsed beneath me, and my feet were in the ground up to my knees. That's why I was sitting—I couldn't stand. I'd sunk into the ground.

"Holy shit," I whispered.

"What were you thinking?" Daniella asked.

"I don't know... I was imagining the ley lines, and then I looked at them, and they were nothing like I'd thought they'd be, and then I was moving along with them," I said.

Deirdre looked shaken, her face pale. "We can't lose you," she whispered.

I took her hand. "You're not going to."

"We almost did."

"Well, let's get me out of here. I'm no longer on ley line duty," I said. I held out my hands.

Dee and Daniella were on one side, and Deirdre and DeAnna on the other. All four pulled, but they couldn't move me. Not an inch.

"Stop!" I yelled. "I don't want to lose a leg, or something equally valuable."

"So what do we do?" Dee asked.

I looked down. The lines were fainter, but they were still there. "Can you still see them?"

"A little," Deirdre said. "Not much."

"OK, good. I'm glad it's not just me. I'm already a little freaked out as it is," I said. "Let me try something." I closed my eyes. Saw the green gray lines, and felt the swoop as I flew along with them.

I have to stop, I thought. *I need to be here.*

I felt a pull, a protest of the wind, of the earth.

I'll come back, I thought. *But my work is here.*

The pull lessened.

I need something. I need the demon spirit.

Anger, white and hot, raged through me.

I opened my eyes, and I was free.

"What did you do?" DeAnna asked.

"I don't know, really," I said, grabbing onto Daniella for support. I sure as hell didn't want to fall on my face.

The green lines pulsed with flashes of white and I knew that whatever had been left at the junction pissed off the energy something fierce.

I closed my eyes, and carefully knelt down. *I'll take it*, I thought. *Get it away from you.*

I flew backwards, right on my ass.

In my arms was an old brown bottle, like the kind they used to sell whiskey in.

"Did you see that?" Deirdre whispered.

I got up, still shaky, clutching the bottle. When Daniella reached for it, I hugged it tighter. "One more thing," I said.

I knelt down again, and put my free hand on the line, which was growing fainter. *Show me*, I thought. *What did you give me?*

Images rushed through my head, so fast and sharp my head ached. There was a demon—I recognized the horns. Not my pain in the ass demon, but a demon. And something white and gold and floaty—and then the demon and the floaty thing tangled. Then the bottle.

I was pushed backwards again. *Thank you,* I

thought. I got to my feet, feeling shaky. The brown bottle was still in my arms.

"We need to leave," I said.

"Are you all right?" Deirdre asked.

"I don't know what I am. But we need to leave. The lines are done."

Thank the Goddess no one questioned me. Instead, they helped me get down the hill, and we piled back into Deirdre's Jeep.

"What was that?" Daniella turned around to look at me from the passenger seat. I was in between Dee and DeAnna, still holding the bottle.

"Did you guys feel it?" I asked.

"I felt something. It was big, and powerful."

"Nature magic," said Deirdre.

I nodded. "I got that, too."

"Why did it suck you into the ground?" Dee asked.

"I was with it, whatever it was," I said. "It was like flying. Like a bird up too high." That was totally inadequate for what I'd felt, but it was the closest I was going to get.

"What's the bottle?" DeAnna asked.

"So I asked it what this was. It showed me something that looked like a demon, and a floating magic looking person thing, and then that was it."

"No sarcophagus?" Deirdre asked.

"Maybe that's just a legend," I said. "Whatever the hell this thing is, this is real. The ley lines were pissed it was there, too."

"Really? How could you tell?" Deirdre was trying not to turn around and stare at the bottle.

"Eyes on the road. We don't want to die the statistical five miles from home," I said. "And I could tell because the ley lines were pissed, like flashing white and I could feel rage."

"That is interesting," Dee said.

"Maybe we don't share this on the message boards," Daniella said with a look at Deirdre.

"Are you sure I can't even share a little?" Deirdre asked.

"No. Whatever this is, we don't need every supernatural in the vicinity coming to look for it." I was firm on that.

"How can we tell what's in it?" Dee asked. "Open it?"

"No!" Deirdre, Daniella, and I all shouted.

"Goddess, no," I said in a normal tone. "Never open something up when you don't know what's in it. That's how you blow yourself and all the shit around you sky high."

"Worst case," Deirdre said. "Best case, just your eyebrows."

Which made us all laugh.

"You scared me," Deirdre said. "I thought you were just going to sink into the ground."

"I could have," I said. "It was that amazing." I knew then, if I ever decided to die, to end my life, that's where I would go. Back to the Earth, back to the energy that circled her. But I didn't say that out loud. I could tell the whole thing had kind of spooked everyone. It had spooked me, too. It would have been so easy to let it take me. It felt that wonderful and intoxicating.

I could never go up there again. I knew, better than most, that when something was that powerful, there was always a price. That much power would demand a high price.

"So how do we see what's in it?" DeAnna asked.

"Witches, remember? We magic stuff," I said, making everyone chuckle.

I'd never been so glad to see Pearl Street. The lights were on downstairs, and when we came into the kitchen, Beeval was sitting on a chair at the island.

"Where's Evil?" I asked him, giving him a one armed hug. I was still holding the bottle.

Beeval drew back from me. "What you have in there, Desimo?" he asked.

"What?" I said.

"There," Beeval pointed at the bottle.

"I don't know," I said. "Something magic? Maybe a demon?"

Beeval scooted off the chair and circled around me, looking like a cat investigating something new. "Demon, yes. Something more."

"Beeval, hang on," I said. I set the bottle on the floor. "What do you see?"

"Demon, other magic. Not demon, something... something more," Beeval said. He leaned down and sniffed the bottle. "Old. This demon old. Used to be angry, now tired."

"How can you tell?" I asked, fascinated.

"Demons know demons," he said.

"Can we open it?" I asked. "Or should we leave it closed?"

Beeval looked at me, and then back at the bottle. He put a hand on it, and his large eyes closed, then snapped back open. "Open. Make promise."

"What do you want me to promise?" I asked.

"No. Make bottle demon promise. Not hurt. No harm."

"Ah, got it." I looked up at my sisters. "We need to get ready."

"You really want to open this?" Daniella was skeptical.

"Beeval, is it safe?" I turned to our demon again.

"No demon ever totally safe. Demons," Beeval shrugged. "But when help given, demons grateful." He smiled then, and the frisson of unease I'd felt when he said no demons were ever safe melted away.

"Let's go out in the back yard," Daniella said.

"No," Beeval said. "Here, your place. Demon know your place, who free."

I think I got it. If we freed the demon, she or he would be grateful, and they would know it was us, and that would keep us safe.

"You're sure?" Deirdre asked Beeval.

He nodded, his large ears flopping.

It was good to have a demon in the house.

The bottle was corked, and there was a wax seal over the cork. The wax was so old that it had turned black.

"Tell demon, no break. No mess. Behave," Beeval said.

The thought of telling a demon to settle down tickled me. I had to hold back a laugh. "Do we just tell it?" I said quietly to Beeval.

He nodded again.

"All right, person in the bottle," I raised my voice. "I'm going to open it, but you need to be calm, and not break up my house. Got it?"

The bottle didn't move, shimmy, shake, nothing.

"Well, that was great," Deirdre said.

"Demon hear," Beeval said. "You open."

"Holy hell, I can't believe we're doing this," DeAnna muttered.

"That makes five of us," Daniella replied.

I got up and got a knife and corkscrew from the kitchen to break the wax. It broke off easily after I managed to get a piece off. Then I put the corkscrew in, and started to ease the cork out.

Whatever was in the bottle was ready to go, because I could feel a vibration, almost like a humming, where my hands touched the body of the bottle.

As the cork came out, the bottle shot out of my hands, and I was falling back again. This was not my day for staying off my ass.

A dark cloud shot up toward the ceiling, swirling faster and faster as it drew down to a smaller cloud until a form took shape.

It was a demon. It was a female demon. She wore a vest of armor over a shapely chest. Her hair was long and black and horns came up through her hair on the top of her head. She had on a wide belt, and I could see the tang of a knife in the belt. But that was where the demon stopped. Below the belt, her dark red skin faded to smoke, the way that you'd think of a genie.

"Who are you?" she asked.

Her voice, although deep, was musical. I mean, for a demon. I'd only met three, and two of them were jerks.

"The Nightingales," I said. May as well get all of us on her good side.

"Why have you freed me?"

"Do you want to go back into the bottle?" I asked. "Should I have left you there?"

"No," she said.

"Who are you?" Deirdre asked.

"I am Catallah, and I have been in the bottle for many moons."

"How'd you end up there?" I asked.

She looked off over our heads, and then down at us. The intensity of her gaze was nearly overwhelming. "I made a mistake. I fell in love."

"Well, love does that kind of thing," Daniella said.

"Indeed, Nightingale. It does. He was not like me, but a djinn, a spirit of the air. It was not allowed."

"I'm sorry," I said, although I wasn't sure anything was really required of me.

"Because of my transgression, my master banished me to the bottle after making me like that which I loved. He said that I should suffer for it, for my boldness and daring."

"Well, that dude was an asshole," I said.

"Yes," Catallah said. "I do not know the word, but the tone in which you speak makes the insult clear."

"Where is he now?" Dee asked. Her eyes were wide.

I got it. I felt a bit overwhelmed myself.

"My master? Or my love?"

"Either?" Daniella said.

"I would wish my master far from here. My love..." she stopped. "I do not know."

"Could you find him?" I asked.

"I am tied to the bottle. I am yours to command, in the way of the djinn."

"What? No!" I said. "I don't—I mean, I'm flattered," I didn't want to offend her.

"Bottle demon go free," Beeval said.

When I'd opened the bottle, he ducked behind the island. Now he came out.

Catallah narrowed her eyes and floated upwards upon seeing Beeval. "Why is the demon here?"

Beeval puffed out his chest. "My home. I live here with Desimo."

Catallah turned her gaze to me. "You are Desimo?"

"Desdemona," I said.

She nodded. "And you opened your home to a demon?"

"He saved me," I replied.

She looked between Beeval and I, and then around. "But you are human."

"Yeah, well, we're all in the same boat," I said.

"What boat?" Catallah looked around.

"Never mind. It's just an expression. Listen, you can stay here if you want, but if you'd rather go find your guy, you can leave." I shrugged. "If you stay, though, you can't trash the place and you have to get along with the ghosts, and not eat the chicken."

"I have a choice?" Catallah asked.

"Sure," I said.

"I need to think on it, Desdemona Nightingale. May I return to the bottle?"

"If that's what you want. You want me to leave the top off?"

Catallah gazed at me for what seemed like a long time. "Yes," she said. Then she whooshed in a puff of smoke back into the brown whiskey bottle.

No one spoke.

"Well. That was..." Daniella said.

"Interesting," Deirdre finished.

"That was holy shit," I said.

Beeval leaned over, patted the bottle, patted me on the head, and walked out of the kitchen.

"I think I'm going to lie down," I said.

"Take her with you," Deirdre said.

"OK. Only wake me up if we're on fire," I replied. Anything else, I didn't care about. I picked up the bottle, which felt warm, and trudged back up to my room. Even though it was still daylight, I set the bottle on my nightstand, and crawled into bed.

I hadn't thought about Zane since this morning.

I thought that might be a good thing.

I ignored the few tears that slid down my face.

Then I closed my eyes and stopped thinking.

CHAPTER FOURTEEN

I opened my eyes to a darkened room. I had no idea what day it was, but I got up, grabbed Catallah's bottle, although I couldn't tell why, and went downstairs.

DeAnna and Dee were huddled around Dee's phone, and Dee was crying. Deirdre and Daniella stood together, arms around each other's waists. Doc was hovering near the stove.

"What's going on?" I whispered.

"All right, please let me know," Dee said, choking on her words as she wiped her eyes. She hung up and began dialing someone else.

"What is going on?" I asked again.

Daniella shushed me.

"Deana!" she shouted.

There was a silence as Dee waited, listening. Then, "Oh, my goddess, Deana, are you all right?"

Another silence.

"I just got a call from the police," Dee said, and then she burst into tears.

Daniella stepped over to Dee and took the phone. She hit a button on it and said, "Deana, you're on speaker."

"Hang on, I think I need to pull over," Deana said. We could hear noise in the background, and then it got quieter. "Okay, I'm back. What's happened?"

"The house in Venice is gone," DeAnna said, wiping her eyes. "The police called, and told us it was on fire, and it burned to the ground."

"What?" Deana whispered, "How?"

"They don't know," DeAnna said. "They told us they couldn't tell if anyone was in there. Dee told us about your call the other day, but she didn't know the details. Are you all right?"

"That utter bastard," Deana practically growled.

"Who?" we all shouted.

"Alfonso Delgado. This is his doing. I'd bet Baby on it."

"You're that sure?" Dee said.

"Who is Baby?" I asked.

"My car," Deana said. "My wonderful car, which was not in the house when it blew up. No, I'm not there. I am on the road, and I'll let you know where I am a little later."

"Are you on the run?" Deirdre asked.

"Apparently so." Deana sounded pissed. "I thought

it would be a good idea to get the hell out of Dodge, so to speak, since I thwarted the plans of Delgado, but now he's upped the stakes."

"You know," I said slowly, "we might be able to buy you some time."

"How?" Dee and DeAnna spoke together.

"Now that we know you're safe, you get to wherever. We'll call you back when we have some idea of whether this can work," I said. "Stay safe, Deana."

"Love you," Deana said. She had grasped Meema's rule from the first time she heard it. She never hung up or left without saying it. I loved this girl.

"Love you," we all said back to her.

Dee hung up, and turned to me. "What's your idea?"

"We need to let everyone know that our niece, our beloved niece, is dead. And after she solved a mystery for Alfonso Delgado, too. Just when she thought she was able to move on, and now the house is gone, she is gone. I think there was a vampire staying there, too. We need to get moving."

"I'm missing something entirely," DeAnna said.

"Yes, you are, but it's all right," I said. "I need to make some calls."

"Des?"

I turned around to see Deirdre looking at me. "What?"

"You going to carry that thing around?" She gestured at the bottle.

I'd forgotten I was carrying it. "Yes. I think I am."

"Well, all right. But if it starts feeling weird, put it down, OK?"

"I will," I said. "Stop worrying. Hey," I said, as a thought struck me. "Has anyone seen Zane?"

"Not since he came by to cancel last night," Daniella said.

"That's not a great sign," I said. "No, don't look at me like that."

Dee was looking reproachful.

"He's up to something, and he didn't tell me, and he broke a date. So... I have to be real. Something's up. It's probably not anything good for us."

"That's pretty pessimistic," DeAnna said.

"Well, it's true," I said. "We'll see when he comes by again." I felt energized as I went back upstairs and pulled out my cell phone.

An hour later, I came back downstairs.

"Well?" Daniella said.

"There will be a body at the house. We will have it brought back here, and we'll throw the biggest wake Deadwood's ever seen. Bigger than Meema's," I said. "We're going to make a huge fuss. And drop lots of hints about this Alfonso Delgado guy. So that everyone knows he was responsible."

"We don't know it was him," Daniella said.

"Do you think Deana is wrong?" Dee asked.

"No, just saying that we don't know."

"Well, if it was him, he'll do something to prove it wasn't. If it wasn't him, he'll be outraged, carry on about his honor, blah blah blah," I said. "Either way, we'll get a sense of things."

"Then what?" Dee asked. "We have no home anymore." Her voice dropped, and she looked like she was about to cry again.

"Yes you do," I said. "You have a home with us always. This way, having the funeral here, and you two moving in, you don't even have to go back there. You'll be safer," I finished.

"You don't mind having us here?" DeAnna asked.

Seeing my nieces, who were well on their way to being like sisters to me, brought so low by the vicious act of some petty vampire made me so angry I could have spit nails.

"We love having you here," Daniella said.

"I was trying to figure out how to ask you to move in," Deirdre said. "Without offending you."

"Really, what is there to go back to?" I asked. "Deana's not there anymore, and she's safe. We're here. So you should be here, too."

Dee and DeAnna burst into tears, and we all spent a little time crying and talking and planning.

But first, we had to get our shit together, and get Deadwood back on the rails.

Daniella got to work planning the funeral. Deirdre went online, posting in great detail and with much flowery language about the loss of our niece.

And I started building her a new life. She couldn't

be Deana Holliday anymore. Not if a vampire was willing to torch her house to keep her quiet, or whatever it was he was after. She needed an entirely new identity.

We worked through the day, and Dee and DeAnna took turns cooking. I was glad to see them taking it easy —they had just lost everything. Although they had us, to lose your entire base—that was tough.

By the end of the day, all the things we needed for Deana were in motion. I sat on the couch in the front room, tired but happy. I hadn't thought about Zane all day. I looked down to see that I was still carrying the brown whiskey bottle.

This was getting weird. As though she knew I was thinking about her, Catallah whooshed up out of the bottle, startling everyone. Dee let out a little yelp of surprise.

"Hey," I said. "What's up?"

"I have been considering your offer," Catallah said. "I would like to be free."

"OK, you're free," I said.

"As the mistress of the bottle, you must wish it so."

It took me a moment, but then I got it. "Ah. OK. Well. OK. Catallah, I wish that you were freed from the bottle."

There was a wind that came out of nowhere, whirling through our front room and kitchen, and it wrapped around Catallah. Then the bottle next to me cracked in two.

The wind disappeared as quickly as it had appeared.

"Is that it?" I asked.

Catallah smiled, and I saw that she had fangs. Like a vampire, only far more scary. "Yes, it is done. I am free."

"Will you be all right? What are you going to do?" I asked. "I meant what I said. You can stay here."

There was a strangled sound from what I thought was one of my sisters, but I couldn't see who it was.

Catallah smiled, and the intensity of her gaze lessened. "I thank you, Desdemona Nightingale, and all the Nightingales. I am in your debt. Because I do not wish to remain so, I shall grant you three wishes."

"Can you do that, without, you know, the bottle or whatever?" Deirdre asked.

"I can do as I please," Catallah said, and there was no mistaking the satisfaction in her tone.

"We don't—" I began.

"Yes, we do," Daniella said.

"What?" I asked. "Can my sisters speak for me?" I asked Catallah.

"Are they Nightingales?" the demon djinn asked.

"They are."

"Then they make make a wish in your name," Catallah said. "If you agree."

"I agree," I said, looking to Daniella. "What do you want?" I couldn't think of anything.

"I would like to ask that you make life difficult for a vampire named Alfonso Delgado," Daniella said. "He has tried to hurt a Nightingale, and he needs to pay for that."

Catallah nodded. "It will be done. Do you have a particular price you wish him to pay?"

"I want his life to suck," Daniella said.

"Then it will."

A thought hit me. "I have a wish!" I said.

"What is it?" Catallah asked.

"Can you make a sarcophagus, a coffin, and make it look enchanted forever? It doesn't have to be magic, but it has to fool a magic user."

"Oh, that's good," Deirdre said.

"So you wish a box that human put their dead in to be enchanted to look like it is magic, but to not actually be magic?" Catallah's brows came together.

"I do. I want to keep someone busy forever," I said.

"That is an odd request, but yes, I can do that."

"You know, we could manage that," Daniella said.

"We don't have demon magic," I said in an undertone. "This thing needs to fool Brian Earl DeGroate to the point that he leaves Deadwood."

"He might not leave alone," Daniella warned.

That's when I knew I wasn't the only one thinking that something had gone badly awry with Zane. That maybe he wasn't who he had presented himself to be.

What if it was all a ruse? To find the sarcophagus?

Well, if it was, then I'd rather know.

"I know that," I said.

"I think the box should also mess with the magic of the person who has it," Deirdre said.

"That will be a third wish," Catallah said.

"That's fine with me," I said. "We can handle everything else. But—"

"Yes?" Catallah asked.

"Can you add onto that third wish? Not only will the owner's magic falter, but the owner of the box cannot be within one hundred miles of Deadwood."

Catallah was quiet for a few moments, thinking. "Yes, I can do this. That will be all of your wishes. Is that acceptable to you?"

"Absolutely," I said.

"I would like to take some time to craft this death box," Catallah said.

"Would a day work?" I asked.

"That would be acceptable. I shall return with the box." The air around us made a whooshing sound, and she was gone.

"That was great, wishing for Delgado's life to suck," I said to Daniella. "Good thinking. I couldn't think of anything at first."

"Well, he deserves it. The final death is too good for him," Daniella said.

"I agree," Dee said fiercely. "Thank you for doing that."

"No problem. Desdemona's right. We don't really need anything else. But what's the box for?" Daniella looked between me and Deirdre.

"We're going to let DeGroate trade us for it."

"How?" DeAnna asked.

"We tell him we found it. And we'll give it to him if he leaves Deadwood."

"Even if Zane goes with him?" Daniella asked.

"No!" DeAnna said. "Zane wouldn't go with that man!"

"He's been scarce around here," I said. "I don't want to think it either, but it could happen. I'd rather be prepared, and give him the choice."

"I don't believe it," DeAnna said. "I won't."

"I hope you're right," I said. Even though whatever it was between us didn't seem destined to make it, I didn't want to think he was like his father. He couldn't be. I could still hear him talking about his mother. No one could fake that.

"OK, so that takes care of DeGroate and Delgado and hopefully our zombie outbreak," Deirdre said. "That leaves Mariah Connors."

"That keeps getting pushed back," I said. "And I really want to find out what we can."

"That's what we'll work on tomorrow, then," said DeAnna. "The funeral is ready, and you've got everything for Deana?" That was directed at me.

I nodded.

Dee gasped.

"What?" Multiple voices asked.

"The cappuccino maker!"

"What?" I asked. "What did I miss, here?"

DeAnna looked at her, and then started to laugh. She laughed so hard that eventually she began to cry, and Dee joined her. Deirdre, Daniella and I watched, mystified.

Finally, the two of them were able to calm down, both wiping their eyes.

"We have this amazing cappuccino maker. It's a tall copper cylinder, and it makes the best coffee ever." Dee sighed.

"There's no way it made it through a house fire," DeAnna said. "But we can find one online."

"Damn it all," Dee said. "I loved that thing. That's the thing I've been missing since we've been here."

"I'm sure we can find you one," I said. As a tea drinker, I didn't get the coffee devotion. But I understood needing that certain something in the morning.

DeAnna hugged Dee.

For the first time in what felt like ages, we sat, talked, and did a whole lot of nothing. We went to bed early, and while I didn't fall asleep with a smile on my face, I had a level of contentment.

We were pulling our lives back together. Which was the most important thing.

CHAPTER FIFTEEN

The next morning, I was up early. It seemed like finally making choices versus having to react to whatever was happening had energized everyone, and I was not the first one downstairs.

We ate together, talking quietly, and by silent agreement, went over to the table where the laptops had been left the night before. We'd been working about an hour when there was a whooshing noise above us that pulled all the air in the room toward the ceiling. It felt weird.

"There's got to be a better way for her to show up," Deirdre muttered.

"Shhh," I said.

Catallah appeared. "I have created the box you requested, Desdemona Nightingale. It will seem to be magic, and whomever possesses it will suffer in the use of their craft. Will that suffice?"

"That's perfect," I said. "It needs to entice a necromancer."

"One enamored of the dead?" Catallah's nose wrinkled.

It was one of the oddest things I'd ever seen, and it made her look less foreign. "That's one way to put it," I said.

"Would you like to see it?" she asked.

I nodded.

Everyone else got up from the table.

Catallah waved her hand, and a small coffin of dark wood appeared. It looked old, older than anything you'd find in a cemetery in Deadwood. It was perfect.

"Touch it," Catallah said.

I stepped close, and laid my hand on the top. The box rattled, and a glow emitted from the box.

"I'd think something live was in there," Dee said, leaning down to peer at it.

"That's the goal. Now we just have to find DeGroate," Daniella said.

"We need to talk to Zane," I said.

"Does the box suit?" Catallah asked.

"Yes, it does. Thank you. Consider that wish fulfilled," I said.

"You cannot see the effect on magic, but it is there." She looked a little anxious.

"I trust you."

"Thank you, Desdemona Nightingale. And I have put things into motion that will allow for the vampire

Delgado to suffer. That may take longer," Catallah said.

"As long as he's perpetually annoyed, I'm good," Deirdre said.

Catallah smiled, showing her fangs. "He will be."

"Then we may consider our bargain fulfilled," I said formally. I had no idea if this was the way, but Catallah seemed a formal kind of demon.

"I would request that I might visit you again, should I be in this part of the world?" Catallah asked.

"You're welcome anytime," I said. I didn't look at my sisters, knowing how they felt about me inviting demons. But hell, I'd brought Beeval in, and he was a gem. I had a feeling about Catallah that I didn't think had anything to do with my carrying her bottle around for two days.

"I thank you, Nightingales. For my freedom, for my welcome. I go to find my love."

"What will you do if you don't find him?" DeAnna asked.

An expression crossed Catallah's face that was so stark I had to look away.

"I am not sure, Nightingale daughter. I am no longer welcome in my clan. I am not demon, nor djinn."

"You're welcome here," I said again.

Catallah inclined her head.

"Good luck," Deirdre said.

The air swirled, and then the demon djinn was gone.

"Wow," Daniella said. "Our days are just getting stranger and stranger."

"We are *not* the home for lost demons," Deirdre said.

"No, we're not," I said. "But Beeval was a great choice to invite in, and I feel like she was, too."

"I agree," said Dee.

"You do?" Deirdre turned to her. "Why?"

"I just have a feeling," Dee nodded.

Deirdre sighed. "It's hard to argue against your feelings, Dee. They've all been pretty accurate."

"I know," said Dee, a smug look on her face.

"All right, all right. I'll stop. But if anything goes sideways, I get to say 'I told you so,'" Deirdre said.

"Deal," I grinned at her. "Even though you're going to lose."

She rolled her eyes, and we went back to work.

After ten minutes, Daniella cleared her throat. "You need to go see Zane, Des."

"Why?" I asked, without looking up from my screen.

"Because you do. Worst case, you get some closure," Deirdre stated.

"Thank you, Dr. Deirdre," I rolled my eyes.

No one else said anything, and I risked a glance. They were all giving me side eye, looking but trying to look like they weren't looking. Dee caught my eye, and nodded.

This was a change. I wasn't used to what could be called TLC from my sisters, from this household. But everyone was being very, very kind about the whole Zane situation.

"OK, I'm going over there now. I'm going to tell him that we were still working on the ley lines thing, and we found the damn box. And I'm going to ask him to make the offer to his dad."

"I'll go with you," DeAnna said.

"No, I can do it," I said. "I need to."

But I went and made sure I didn't look like I'd rolled out of bed. Then I squared my shoulders, and walked out the front door to Zane's house.

"Morning, Mrs. Kittrick," I said to our elderly neighbor. Her cats, Tinky and Winky, were out in the garden with her, and I could swear that one of them winked at me.

Mrs. Kittrick nodded, and then shuffled over to the fence that divided our yards. "I saw the notice about your cousin in the paper. Deana? That was her name?"

I'd forgotten that we were throwing a funeral and a wake tomorrow. After all, that was tomorrow. We still had to get through today. "Yes, that was her."

I moved toward the fence since all signs pointed toward Mrs. Kittrick wanting to chat.

"I'm sorry, Desdemona. This has been a tough month for you girls."

If I hadn't been partially leaning on the fence, I might have fallen over. For as long as I could remember, Mrs. Kittrick had referred to us as the Nightingale... women. With that very pregnant pause before the word women. As though she wanted to call us something far less savory.

"Yes, ma'am, it has," I said. "Deana was a great girl."

Mrs. Kittrick nodded. "I'm very sorry. I'll see you tomorrow at the church." And with another nod, she shuffled back toward her porch.

Holy shit. The axis of the earth must be shifting. I might have to stop gunning it in the 911 as I passed her house. I continued my walk, and when I was in front of Zane's house, I took a deep breath, and walked up to the front door. I knocked firmly.

Then I waited.

Maybe he wouldn't be here, and I could avoid this a little longer. I wasn't being a coward, it just meant I didn't have to put the idea of a partner who got it—got me—to bed quite as soon.

The door swung open, and Zane filled the doorway. His hair stood up in spikes, and he had stubble across his perfect jawline. He looked as though he hadn't been sleeping.

"I'm sorry about the other night," he said.

I shrugged, keeping my expression calm. "These things happen," I said. "I came to see you because I have some news. Are you in touch with your father?"

His expression shifted and he very nearly hunched over. "I have been."

"Well, of course you have. Listen, you need to get in touch with him. We found the sarcophagus."

"You're kidding," Zane stood up, shocked.

Uh, huh, I thought. Now you're all into this conversation.

"We did. And we'll give it to him—"

"Are you sure you want to do that?" he asked. "That may not be the wisest choice."

I held up a hand. "We'll only give it to him if he leaves Deadwood."

"He's going to try and take it from you," Zane said.

"He can try," I grinned. The thought of a fight was a good one.

"If he does agree, he'll try and cheat."

"He can try," I said again. Like we hadn't come across this kind of guy before. I resisted the urge to scoff, to do a little trash talking. That wasn't the point. I wanted the guy to come to us, hand out, wanting the sarcophagus. "Can you let him know?"

"Yes," he said, and there was a lot in that one word.

"Great. Come by if you find him, and he wants to make a deal." I turned on my heel and walked away.

I don't know if Zane was staring, but I hoped so. Once I heard the door close, I hurried back to our place.

"Listen," I burst through the door. "We need to be ready for DeGroate today. He'll be here, and I want to force him to make a magical bargain with us."

"Perfect," Daniella said. "If he breaks it, we own him."

"We already own him," I said.

"What happened with Zane?" DeAnna asked.

I noted that my sisters stopped, wanting to hear my answer.

"Nothing. He told me he was sorry he had to bail, and then we talked about his dad. He said his dad would try to cheat us in every way he could."

"Well, of course he will." Daniella shrugged. "Big deal. We can handle that."

"Did he say anything else?"

"Nope. Not a thing."

"Really?" Deidre said. "I'm so disappointed in him."

"These things happen," I said. "Let's get ready for Daddy Dearest. We need to leave him no way out except the way we want him to go."

Two hours later, there was a knock on the door.

"Showtime," I said.

Dee went to the door, and Zane and Brian Earl DeGroate stood on the porch.

"I told my dad about your offer," Zane said. "Can we come in?"

"Yes," Daniella said.

"I want to see the sarcophagus," DeGroate said. His eyes were hungry.

Perfect.

"We'll get to that," I said calmly.

"How did you find it?"

"We followed your lead," Deirdre said. "Zane found the zombie at the mine site, and then your comments about ley lines, combined with a little research, and we were able to find it."

"I don't believe you," DeGroate said flatly.

"Believe what you want. We have ways of finding the information we seek," Daniella said.

DeGroate crossed his arms. "My son tells me that you are seeking to make a bargain. A trade, as it were."

"We are," I said. "We will give you this sarcophagus—"

"Have you opened it?"

I rolled my eyes. "We don't open things when we're not sure what is in there."

It was DeGroate's turn to roll his eyes. He was sure he knew what was in there. What he didn't realize was that we'd saved his ass. Catallah would have had him for lunch before he could have gotten a wish out or said a word to establish himself as her master.

That's even assuming the ley lines would have given the bottle up for him. As much as the ley lines didn't like having the bottle there, they would not have liked this guy.

"Let me see it," he said again.

"Dad," Zane said.

"Be quiet, boy," DeGroate said. "You've done your part. Now let me do mine."

What the hell was Zane's part? I glared at him, unable to help myself. He met my eyes and looked away.

Damn it.

"You will need to made a bargain with us that is sealed by magic," I said.

"Do not dictate to me, girl," DeGroate said.

How in the hell had no one kicked this guy's teeth in? Then I remembered that most necromancers were solitary sorts, and didn't interact with people much. Which meant that he probably had no idea how he sounded.

That didn't mean I liked him any better.

"Since I have what you want, I think I'm in a good position to bargain as I wish." I gave him eyeball for eyeball.

No one moved.

Then DeGroate sighed. "What are you offering?"

"We'll give you the box, and you leave Deadwood. Take any of your zombies with you, or leave us the location of any you have with you still, and we'll put them to rest."

"And you will give me the box and let me leave?" His eyebrows went up.

Zane stood off to the side of his father, arms crossed, not looking at any of us.

"Yes."

"Do you have any idea what's in the sarcophagus?"

"We do," Deirdre said. "But even if it's true, we don't have need of such a thing."

DeGroate snorted, not bothering to hide his disdain for such an idea.

I saw Dee frown at him. I hoped she would not say anything. This was going exactly the way I wanted.

"Then why is it you're forcing me to bargain with you?" DeGroate was pissed.

I hid a smile. "Because we would like you to leave Deadwood."

DeGroate pulled himself up. "That may not be what I wish to do."

I shrugged. "That is certainly your choice. However, I will not allow you to have the box unless you agree, via magical bargain, that you will be leaving immediately."

"I could take the sarcophagus." DeGroate's eyes narrowed as he regarded me.

"You could try," I said softly. I didn't say another word. I waited. Part of me wanted him to do something, make a move. A fight would be the perfect thing right now.

"I will make your bargain," DeGroate said. His voice was full of suppressed anger.

"You will swear," I said.

"I will," he replied.

I held out my hand, and Brian Earl DeGroate took mine.

"You will leave Deadwood immediately. In exchange for your word to do so, you will receive the sarcophagus that we found. Do you agree?" I asked.

"I agree," he said.

The magic held our hands together for a moment, and then dissipated.

"It's done. DeAnna, would you bring out the sarcophagus?"

DeAnna nodded, and went into the kitchen to bring it out from behind the island.

DeGroate's eyes widened, and I saw him realize that it had been in his grasp the entire time. His eyes flew to me, full of anger and the desire to lash out, but one look at me, and my sisters behind me, and he mastered himself.

Good thing. He didn't know how badly I wanted to pick a fight. But this was Zane's father, no matter what he did or said. Nothing would change that.

Zane still wasn't meeting my eyes, or anyone else's.

DeAnna held the box out to DeGroate, who took it with barely restrained greed. Whatever else he'd been feeling, he was beyond it now, with his sarcophagus in hand.

"Zane," DeGroate said, "It's time to leave."

I looked at Zane, and I knew my mouth must have fallen open.

DeGroate laughed. "Did you think he would forget that he was my son?"

I didn't speak.

"You've insisted that I pay your price. Now you must pay mine. Zane is my son, and he will be leaving with me."

"Zane?" I asked.

"Zane is leaving," DeGroate said. He turned, box in hand, and walked to the door.

I looked at Zane. It was all a lie. All of it. Everything he'd said, done—a lie. I felt something break in me at the thought.

Zane stared at me, and Goddess help me, I couldn't tell what he was thinking.

"Dad," Zane said, "have a good trip. Don't come back."

DeGroate turned so quickly I thought he might hurt himself. "What are you talking about?"

"This is my home, Dad. You're not welcome here because you showed up and tried to shit all over my home. You've treated my friends poorly, and even now that you've gotten what you wanted, you're still behaving badly. You need to leave."

"I should have never given you a chance," DeGroate sneered.

"No, I shouldn't have given you a chance," Zane snapped. He strode to the door and yanked it open. "You made a bargain. You need to honor it."

"You will regret this," DeGroate hissed as he walked out our front door.

"I already am," Zane replied. After his dad walked out, he slammed the door shut. Then he turned, his focus on me. "I'm sorry. I've been trying to get him to leave. I had to cancel. I didn't want him to know that... well, I didn't want him to know anything more than he already did. He uses everything he can."

I didn't speak.

"Desdemona?" Zane said.

Dee walked up to him and slapped him in the face. "You need to go home, Zane," she said.

Zane was astounded. Not only due to the slap, the crack of which echoed around the room, but that he wasn't instantly forgiven. He looked to all of us.

Every one of us stood with stony faces.

"Go home, Zane," Daniella said.

Through it all, I didn't say anything. I'd crossed my arms when he started to explain, and hadn't moved since. I didn't know what I felt, but forgiving sure as hell wasn't it. I turned, and walked to the stairs, making my thoughts plain without saying a word.

"I'm sorry. You need to know that. I'm sorry."

I heard footsteps, and then the door shut softly.

"He's gone," DeAnna said.

I came back down the few steps. "Dee, I wasn't expecting that."

Dee smiled, but it was a sad smile. "He's a good guy, but he has been stupid, stupid, stupid. If you decide to let him back in, he needs to make up for it."

"I don't know what to think," I said.

"He could have told us what he was doing. It's not like we're amateurs. We can handle a Brian Earl DeGroate any day," Daniella sniffed.

"She's right," Deirdre said, looking at me. "We're with you, whatever you want."

"Thanks," I said. "I don't know, yet."

"You don't have to," Dee said.

I smiled at my family.

"That was the slap heard round the world," Doc drifted in from the kitchen.

I wondered where it was he hung out that he was always coming in right next to the stove.

"You saw it?" Dee asked.

"I see everything, darlin'," Doc said.

"That is the beginning of a horror show," Deirdre rolled her eyes.

I laughed. "A couple of months ago, I would have hated to hear that," I said. "Now I'm OK with it, despite the fact that you might see more than you bargained for."

"I am a gentleman," Doc said. "No matter what, of that you can be sure."

"I'm not insinuating otherwise," I said. "Where's Granny?"

"We do not spend all our time together. And she's not as zen with her afterlife as I am," Doc said.

"Easy, smart ass," Daniella said. "Listen, Des, go to bed. We'll make sure everything's ready for the funeral tomorrow."

"Shit," I said. "I totally forgot."

"Well, we've had the agenda from Hell," Dee said.

"It almost feels too—" DeAnna started.

"No!" Deirdre, Daniella, and I all shouted. "Don't!"

"Don't what?" DeAnna looked mystified.

"Don't jinx us," I said. We never commented on how easy things were. It was the death knell to any plans, even well-thought out plans.

DeAnna looked to each of us, and then realization dawned. "Oh. Oh! I'm sorry."

"It's all good," Daniella said. "But we never say that kind of thing."

"Got it," DeAnna said. "The lessons never stop."

"No, they never do. Which isn't a bad thing," I said.

"It's not. Go to bed, Desdemona," DeAnna said. "We got this."

"Thanks," I said. I found that I was tired, and bed sounded like the perfect thing. Normally, I liked to be in the thick of things, but not today.

And honestly, I could feel good about letting someone else take the reins today. We'd stopped our zombie plague. We'd kicked the dangerous necromancer out, and kept him from getting a dangerous object. We'd banned him from Deadwood.

He'd try to come back in. They always did. But both the bargain that he made, and the box that Catallah had crafted would kick him right back out.

We'd helped Deana get the hell out of Los Angeles in one piece, and—I turned and went back downstairs.

"We need to call Deana, let her know what we've done," I said. "I forgot about it in the midst of all our demon visits."

Dee called her, and we gave her the details of her new life. Deana was sad that Deana Holliday would be a thing of the past, but after tomorrow, the rest of the world would think she was dead. We had to keep the rest of the world thinking that—which meant that she had to be someone else.

So we'd made someone else for her.

When Dee hung up the phone, despite the tears that everyone had shed during the call, I felt good. One more problem down. Now I could go to bed.

And try not to think about the way my life had gone. It sucked when what you thought was happening didn't.

Part of being a Nightingale. I would shake this off. Eventually.

I had to.

CHAPTER SIXTEEN

I was up early again, up before the sun, and I started the tea kettle. No one else came down, although Doc drifted in.

"How're you doin', darlin'?" Doc asked.

"I'm here. I'm doing. I'm sad, which will work well for today."

"I don't like that we're having a funeral for someone not dead." Doc shook his head.

"We're protecting her," I said.

He shook his head. "Doesn't mean I have to like it."

We were having the service at the same church we'd had Meema's service at. Then we were having the wake, so to speak, at our shop. Normally, I'd be running around like crazy. But my whole family was here, and they'd take care of it.

I made another cup of tea. It was nice. "We really need to find Mariah Connors or her offspring," I said.

"I have a feeling you will," Doc said.

"Did you know her?" I asked.

He shook his head. "With my own illnesses, I stayed away from everyone who might even think about being sick."

"Makes sense," I said.

Deirdre came down the stairs. "You're up early," she said to me. "Morning, Doc."

"Deirdre," Doc said politely. As he always did.

"Ready for today?" Deirdre asked. "It's going to be a long day."

"I know," I said.

"I'll be sure to make a long tribute post to Deana," Deirdre said. "You know, to twist the knife a little." She was referring to Alfonso Delgado, who Deana suspected was behind a great deal of her woes, and the destruction of the Carroll Canal house.

"He sounds perfectly disagreeable," I said.

"All the more reason to annoy him," Deirdre said.

"Because you find yourself light on things to do?" Doc asked, still polite as ever.

Deirdre and I laughed. Doc had a way of breaking things down.

Daniella got up as Dee and DeAnna came downstairs.

Before we knew it, it was time to go to the church. We made it before people started streaming in—I didn't know whether anyone would be there. But people came, because even though Deana hadn't been well known, she was a Nightingale, and she was one of us.

As the church filled, Dee wiped tears away. "This makes me all weepy, people coming because of you three." She spoke in a whisper.

"Nightingales are part of Deadwood," I said.

That only made Dee cry a little more, and I thought part of it might be relief. Either way, it looked totally appropriate.

After that, the day flew by, and as the sun went down, the last of the mourners left our shop. We cleaned up and went back to Pearl Street.

"I'm exhausted," Daniella said.

"But you did great," Deirdre said. "I'll be able to write about this with great detail and feeling."

"It's a good thing we found her a new identity," DeAnna said.

"It will give her time to hide, and to see if anything shakes out now," I said.

The next few days were quiet. We'd closed the shop, and everyone stayed close to home. We made sure to send a package full of new identity items to Deana, who we now needed to refer to as Delilah. DeAnna had come up with that one.

And because we were supposedly in mourning, people let us be.

Even Zane, I noted sadly. He was still in Deadwood, because I saw lights on in his house. I was fairly certain his dad was gone—if the magical bargain hadn't forced the issue, the box we gave him would.

I wondered if anything had gone awry for Brian Earl DeGroate yet; Zane hadn't come down to pound on our door and yell about the unfairness of it all. Part of me wished that he would, just so that I could see him.

Three days after the funeral and wake, there was a knock on the front door after dark.

"Who could that be?" Dee asked.

Doc and Granny were hanging out with us, and they faded back into the woodwork. Literally.

Deirdre went to the door, and Daniella and I were right behind her, magic coiled and ready. I hoped it might be Zane.

As Deirdre opened the door, I was poised to blast anyone not friends.

A woman and two men stood there, all of them holding up their hands.

They were vampires.

"What do you want?" Deirdre asked.

"We come from Alfonso Delgado," the woman said.

Dee and DeAnna got up, and I felt the magic from the five of us moving around. It was mixed with anger and a desire for revenge.

"We should just blast you right now and call it a night," I said.

"Please don't," the woman said. "We come to make peace."

"Are you going to rebuild our home?" DeAnna stepped forward. "Give us back Deana?"

The woman was a cool customer, I'll give her that. "We can rebuild the home."

"You're admitting that you blew it to bits in the first place?" Daniella asked angrily.

"Alfonso admits that he might have known it was happening and he didn't do anything to stop it," the woman said cagily.

Damn vampires.

"And what does that do for us?" Dee asked.

"It doesn't do anything, but Alfonso wanted to express his sorrow at the loss of Deana. He was very impressed with her not only as a Nightingale, but as a witch. She had recently been of service to him."

"Yeah, and he killed her for it," Deirdre said.

"He is very sorry for your loss," the woman said.

I'll give her credit. She was going to get her task done, no matter how uncomfortable it was. "You were right," I whispered to Deirdre, even as I knew the vampires could hear us. I didn't care. Let this crew report back that Alfonso Delgado was on our radar, and not in a good way.

But Deana was right. Making a big deal of this, not hiding it—it had rattled Delgado.

And hopefully he was suffering due to the wish we'd made with Catallah. He was a jerk, and deserved every bit of whatever trouble came to him.

"Why does he send you?" I asked.

"So that you know of his sorrow," the woman kept a straight face, although I wasn't sure how, "and to let you know that he wishes to ease your sorrow. If you need anything of him, he asks that you contact him without delay."

The woman inclined her head. It was a little formal, but vampires tended to be kind of formal. Manners, as I'd told Deana, were important to them.

"We will keep that in mind," I said loftily. It was better that Delgado be unsure about how his offer was received.

"Thank you," the woman said. She and the two men turned around, and they zoomed off into the night.

I waited until I was sure they were gone, holding up a hand so that no one spoke. Vampires had great hearing. Deirdre shut the door, and all five of us burst into laughter.

"Whatever Catallah did to him, combined with everything you've posted online is making him nervous as hell," I said.

"Good," DeAnna said. "He deserves it, the little shit."

"Yes, he does," Daniella said.

It was a small bright spot against a somber week.

Coloring it all for me was the fact that I hadn't seen Zane. Dee whispered to me during the funeral service that he'd been in the back of the church, but I hadn't seen him myself.

Despite it all, that made me sad. Damn it.

But on another small bright spot, we had time to finally, finally track down Mariah Connors. Or what we thought were her descendants. The final big task on our to do list.

"Should we email them?" Daniella asked as we sat around the table together.

"Or will it just piss them off?" Deirdre asked.

"You think they know about Mariah?" Dee asked.

"I'd tell my story to my family if I were her," I said. "Wouldn't you?"

"All right. I'm going to email them," Deirdre said.

"Goddess, go gently," I said. A thrill of fear rushed through me. We'd been operating on the idea that either I was doomed, as one of the Desdemonas, or that those I loved were doomed, given what had happened to Granny, and Meema, and Jack Fitzgerald and our stepfather Burnsie, and maybe even DeAnna, as someone who had been named Desdemona.

Some clarification would be nice.

Although the lack of clarity would be the best curse of all, I realized.

We'd taken off the entire week, and tomorrow was our last day off before we had to be seen to get back to life.

Deirdre sent off a carefully worded email. All there was to do was wait.

Which sucked. I hated waiting. But there was nothing we could do.

This was beyond our control.

Which also sucked.

On our last day off, just after breakfast, there was a knock at the door.

Deirdre and Daniella and I looked at one another, and we moved as one.

"At least it can't be vampires," Daniella said.

"Well, that's one good thing," I agreed.

Slowly, Daniella opened the door.

Two woman were on the porch. They looked to be mother and daughter. Neither were smiling.

"You're looking for us," the older of the women said.

"And you are?" I asked.

"Mariah and Rebecca Connors."

DARK PACT

Dark Pact
Book One
The Mostly Open Paranormal
Investigative Agency

It begins, as it always does, with the best, most friendly, helpful of intentions.

The road to utter Hell, that is.

Isn't that how most people get there?

My aunts in Deadwood might have a different opinion, but they're the exception. Most people didn't have a grandmother making deals with demons. I did. Even though that grandmother (known as Granny) is long gone, her choices live on to plague her descendants.

That's not the point. The point is, here I am, fresh off a tangle with a really immense ass of a demon, and I'm right back in the hot seat of a supernatural tangle.

Let me back up a little bit. That road, the one to Hell? For me, it started with a phone call. On what had already been a weird day.

I'd been back from Deadwood for about two weeks. I'd helped my aunts (who were over one hundred and twenty years old and essentially immortal, as long as they stayed in Deadwood. My great grandmother, also named Deana, had left her sisters and mother and gone to Los Angeles, never to return to Deadwood) defeat a gross demon named Ashlar and discovered just as we took a breath that my aunt Desdemona, and my grandmother, who was originally named Desdemona before she legally changed her name, were both cursed.

Did you get all that? There's a lot of D's in that.

Me being me, I'd insisted that I stay, and help them sort yet another mess out. But all five—all three aunts and my mom and gran—had insisted I come home to Venice.

Before we'd gone to Deadwood for the funeral of my great aunt Meema (the first time I'd ever been to Deadwood, or known much about Great Gran's family), I'd been in the process of opening my private investigative business. I'd gotten my license and had saved enough money to rent a place and open. I even had clients waiting.

So that's what I did. Left Mom and Gran in Deadwood with the aunts who could never die. Opened the Holliday Private Investigations as I'd planned. Everything was going well, going... normally. Until this morning.

This morning, I'd gotten up early and made a pie. I didn't know why, but the pull to get up and bake had been so strong, I hadn't been able to stay in bed. And not just any pie—Smokin' Hawt Cherry Chipotle pie. I'd bought cherries just yesterday on a whim. I had no idea why I had to bake, but I did. I hadn't baked pies since before Derek, my fiancé, had died. Before he died, I baked all the time. And they hadn't even been for Derek. They'd been for one of the members of his band.

One of the things my aunts had emphasized was to listen to my gut. They said now that I knew my history, and had used some of my witch skills, the more I used them, the more they'd grow. Intuition—known as gut instinct—was part of that.

Following my gut, I made the pie, and brought it into work. I cut it into eighths, and waited to see what happened. I couldn't say how I knew something would happen, but I just did. It was my second official day of business. Which is when a call—the call I mentioned earlier—the one that started the road to Hell—came in from my past.

I had no idea as I answered the phone what was coming. Honestly, I was still focused on what the hell the pie and baking urge was all about. "Hello, Holliday Private Investigations, this is Deana, how can I help you?"

A silence and then, "Deana? It's Kel."

I nearly dropped the phone. Kel, formally known as Kelsey Grayson Worthington, was the best friend of my late fiancé, Derek Sinnful (Yes. He really did legally change his name). Derek was the lead singer in Copernicus, and Kel was the drummer. Before Derek died, they were on their way. Since then, they'd gone in a different direction.

So had I. I'd built a lot on being the future Mrs. Sinnful, and it was hard to let go of that. But I'd had to. Derek was gone. I'd lost him.

Derek had been out on a new bike, testing it up in Franklin Canyon park, and someone had hit him, and left him for dead. He hadn't been found until later in the evening. I'd been the one to find him. The cops wouldn't go looking for him, not deeming six hours long enough to be concerned. But I knew something was wrong. I'd known for five of the six hours since he'd left.

I'd just ignored it, telling myself I was worrying too much.

It was because of Derek I'd ended up with my PI license. I wanted to find out who had hit him. So far, nearly three years later, I hadn't. There were no cameras, or any way to trace who'd been in the park that day.

"Kel. It's been a long time. What's up?" I kept my tone level. It was hard. I'd seen Kel every day of my life while Derek and I had been together. He was like family. But after Derek died—everyone fell apart, rather than coming together. Kel and me particularly. I had a particularly large beef with him, but I'd wait to see if I needed to bring that out.

"What kind of investigations do you do?" There was something off in his voice.

"All kinds. What are you looking for?"

His voice lowered to nearly a whisper. "Can I come and see you?"

"Sure. Are you okay?"

"No," he said and hung up.

I sat back in my chair, the thread of worry that had begun when I heard his voice sprouting to full-on worry. I wouldn't have long to wait. He'd be here soon, if he still lived where he had when we'd been friends.

Thirty minutes later, the door swung open, the soft chime I'd installed ringing. Kel came in. He looked at me, and then smiled. "Hey, Dee, how are you?"

I got up and came from around the desk to shake his hand. I wasn't up for a hug. "I'm good."

"This is good to see," he said, gesturing around at my office. "Hey, is that cherry pie?"

Well, isn't this interesting. "It is," I agreed. "But let's not waste time. What's up? You sounded horrible. Have some pie and tell me about it."

He sighed, the smile dropping from his face. He walked to my buffet table where I kept the coffee and today, the pie, put a piece on a paper plate, and sat in the chair in front of my desk. I went back to my chair. This felt bad.

"This is going to sound crazy." He took a bite mechanically. "But thanks for making my favorite pie. I wouldn't have thought you remembered. How did you know I was going to call you today?"

I shrugged. Internally, I thought, Well, shit. Now I know why I was compelled to bake this morning. I wondered if this was going to become a habit—a pie baking frenzy just before someone rolled into my life. I didn't remember that his favorite pie was cherry, but why would I? I'd done my best to forget all about Kel.

"This is delicious, the extra spice or whatever." He took another bite. "But about why I'm here—my situation—this is crazy," he said again.

He had no idea what my crazy meter looked like these days. "I've seen some pretty strange shit. Just spit it out."

"I went out with a witch," he said.

"Really? A witch? That's unusual?" I asked. I couldn't help grinning.

He looked up and glared. "I'm serious."

I wiped the grin off my face. "So am I. Like, a real witch? How do you know?" Since I'm part witch myself, I wondered how one told a boyfriend. I leaned forward, eager to know. Not that there was a boyfriend on the horizon. I was just interested.

"She told me, and well, after she told me, it was pretty obvious. She dealt with some... interesting characters."

"Really?"

He shook his head as he ran a hand through his hair. "We dated for a while, and then we broke up, and I ran into someone I'd met coming in her place. That was even weirder," Kel said, stopping to look over my head.

"How?"

He looked down, away from me. "It sounds crazy to even think it." He seemed stuck as to his choice for words.

"No judgement, Kel. Just tell me."

"Lavina was—is—a vampire."

I sat back. I hadn't been expecting that but given my summer so far, I wasn't entirely surprised. Spending time in Deadwood, learning about my family history, meeting my too many times great-grandfather (Doc Holliday, *the* Doc Holliday, if you please!), and any number of other things that happened during the visit to Deadwood left me less ready to clutch my pearls about the unusual than I'd been earlier in the year.

"Okay," I said. "Is that the bad thing that brings you here?"

Kel looked sheepish. "No, it's great—really great, honestly. I like her a lot." He stopped, taking another bite of the pie. "This is delicious," he said again with his mouth full.

Good grief. I was going to have to pry this out of him. "So what's the problem, Kel?" I asked.

"She got into an argument with another vampire, and now that vampire is dead."

"I don't know—"

"They think I did it!" Kel burst out, leaning forward. He set his plate on my desk. "They took Lavina away to talk to her two days ago, and then last night, three of them showed up at my door and told me I had a week to get my affairs in order and then I was coming with them to stand trial."

"What?" This didn't make sense. It was a huge leap to sleeping with a vampire to becoming a murderer. Not to mention, Kel was—used to be--one of the nicest guys I'd ever met. He was certainly the kindest guy in the band, and I'd been engaged to one of the other guys. Derek had been wonderful, but he wasn't kind like Kel was. Well, like Kel had been. Once Derek died—well, people showed different sides of themselves in death.

"Why do they think you did it?" I asked.

"There's a law against killing other vampires. If you're found guilty, you end up put outside in the daytime, or something like that."

Part of me was just astounded by the fact that I was having this conversation. The practical part of me said, "So they figure Lavina got you, through her feminine wiles, to do her dirty work?"

He nodded. "That's the gist of it. I didn't do this, Deana! You know me!" He picked up the plate again, angrily spearing the pie.

"I did," I said quietly.

He had the grace to look up at me, the fork halfway to his mouth, ashamed. He didn't say anything. What could he say? He was a dick to me when Derek died, and he knew it. He knew I knew it. The fact that I was sitting here talking to him was more of a testament to my feelings for Derek than it was for Kel.

"Look, Deana, I'm sorry—"

I held up a hand to cut off any statements of regret or repentance. They were forced by the situation and empty. "Please don't insult either one of us. Tell me what you want me to do for you, and I'll tell you if I can manage it, and what the price will be."

He paled under his complexion, but he took a breath, and spoke. "I want you to find out who did this. It wasn't me. I wasn't doing anything other than dating a vampire who got into a dust up with another one. That's the only thing I did. Lavina is hot, and sexy, and fun, and I really care about her, but I don't want to die for going out with her."

"Why do you think I can do anything with this?" I asked quietly.

"Because you're the only person I know who does this kind of thing that I can tell the truth to. I'm desperate," he said.

"I figured," I shot back. "How did you know I did this? I've only just opened."

"Look, if you can't help me, just say so," Kel got up. "I was hopeful when I saw your name online."

"I can," I said quietly.

"Are you just saying that? Because I didn't have any idea all these kinds of, of people, existed until this year." He took another bite of pie.

I nodded, thinking it was amazing that this guy was here in my office, and we were having this sort of conversation while he ate. He was telling me he didn't want to die while he snarfed down my baked goods. "I have connections. But it's going to cost you."

His face took on a wary expression. "How much?"

"Just one 1948 Indian Chief motorcycle, formerly the property of Derek Sinnful. If you haven't sold it for parts by now," I said.

Kel sat down holding his plate tightly, his lips also tight.

Why he hadn't expected that when he called me, much less walked in here was beyond me, but it wasn't my problem. Derek had never gotten around to changing his will, and in the will, which was five years old at the time, he'd given Kel everything. But in anticipation of our wedding, he rebuilt the Indian Chief for me, and it had our initials on it. Kel knew this. All he had to do was give me the Indian as Derek had intended.

Instead, he told me that if Derek had wanted to change his will, he would have, and told me he wasn't doing anything outside of what was specified in the will.

He was right. This was Derek's fault. Derek could have changed it. But he got everything—Derek's stuff, his shares in the band, his place—all I wanted was the bike.

And Kel, once the nicest guy I'd ever met, said no, and shut a door in my face. More than once.

"Deana—"

It was my turn to stand. "If you can't manage the terms of what is agreeable to me, I'm sorry, Kel, but I won't be able to take the job. I'll wish you good luck." I took a few steps around the desk.

"I could die."

"My price is reasonable, given the market value," I said, looking out the window. "And since the bike was personalized, that knocks down overall value." These were all facts that Kel knew.

"I sold it for parts."

"Then my fee will be one hundred thousand dollars, upfront," I said.

"What the hell? No way, Deana! You're out of your fucking mind!"

"Maybe." I shrugged. "Sorry I can't help you, Kel. And I am really sorry, because we were good friends at one point, and I don't think you're a horrible person. You're just an asshole to me." I crossed my arms and waited for him to leave. I could cry later. I wouldn't do it in front of Kel Worthington. Not ever again.

He strode to the door and slammed it behind him as he left. I did notice he took the pie with him. Perhaps the baking was a warning sign of what would be walking into my place. Something to think about. Later.

Right now, I went to my desk and put my head down and cried like Derek had just died.

When I went home that night, I was restless, missing my mom and Gran. Tonight, I was wishing they were here. But I couldn't call them, couldn't add on to their burden. They were trying to save their own lives.

Well, I'd been willing to try and save a life, but he just wouldn't let go of the bike. That was on Kel, no matter how guilty I was feeling. I stared at the television, not really watching it when the ring of the doorbell made me jump.

I padded silently to the door. I opened it to find Kel standing under the porch light, hands in pockets. He looked up and saw me, and without saying a word, stretched his right hand out toward me.

I held out my own hand, and he dropped a set of keys into it. "Meet me tomorrow at your office so I can give you all the information," Kel said, his voice flat.

"Title," I said.

He pulled an envelope from his back pocket and held it out to me. I took it.

"I'm sorry, Deana. Sorrier than you know."

"So am I," I said quietly.

We stared at one another, and then he turned and walked away. I waited until I heard his car leave to go out to the garage.

There in the light, was the Indian Chief. *My* Indian Chief. My bike, restored for me by Derek. Gleaming red, as it had been when Derek painted it. I walked over, and let my fingers trail along the leather seat, still stamped with the "DHS" that Derek had commissioned for it. For what would have been my initials after we married.

And on the gas tank, there it was. The bike was red, with black and chrome accents. But right there in pink and white and silver was a heart with two entwined 'D's'. For me and Derek.

Kel hadn't sold it for parts, or painted over it, or done anything other than kept it. And now, it was with me. I cried a little more as I ran my finger over the initials and the heart, remembering watching Derek paint it. It wasn't perfect, but he wanted to do this one thing that made my bike special, as his gift to me. I'd loved it.

I opened the garage and wheeled the bike in next to my FJ Toyota Land Cruiser, affectionately known as Baby. Now I had Baby and the Chief. As I closed the door, I watched as both of my babies disappeared from view.

Then I went in and went to bed, dreaming of fangs gleaming in the dark all night long.

Dark Pact is the first book in the Mostly Open Paranormal Investigative Agency series. Deana is the niece of Desdemona, Deirdre, and Daniella Nightingale. To read more of her story, click HERE.

Lisa Manifold is a *USA Today* Bestselling Author of
fantasy, paranormal, and romance stories. She moved to
Colorado as an adult and has no plans of living
anywhere else. She is a consummate reader, often

running late because "Just one more page!" She is a fan of all things Con, and has an entire room devoted to the costumes created for Cons.

Lisa is the author of many flavors of paranormal series, including The Realm, Djinn Everlasting, Dragon Thief, The Aumahnee Prophecy, Tales from the Veil, Sisters of the Curse, the books from The Midnight Coven collective, the Deadwood Sisters and The Mostly Open Paranormal Investigative Agency.

She lives as close to the mountains as possible with her husband, children, and four red rescue dogs.

Stay in touch:
Sign up for my Newsletter and never miss a thing!
Website: www.lisamanifold.com
Or one of the links below.
Xoxo
Lisa

The Midnight Coven Stories

(books written with a collective of authors)

Cursed Coven Series

Wicked Love (Oct 2019)

Vampire Mates Series

Immortal Darkness

Vampire Brides Series

Forever Blood

The Mostly Open Paranormal

Investigative Agency

Dark Pact

Dark Night (Nov 2019)

Deadwood Sisters

Hellborn: The Unlucky Book 1

Hellfire: The Unlucky Book 2

Hellfury: The Unlucky Book 3 (Dec 2019)

Dragon Thief

Dragon Lost

Dragon Found

The Realm Series

Heart of the Goblin King

To Wed the Goblin King

Realms of the Goblin King

Rise of the Dragon King

The Companion Tales, Volume I

The Companion Tales, Volume II

The Aumahnee Prophecy

with Corinne O'Flynn

Eamonn's Tale

Marigold's Tale

Watchers of the Veil

Defenders of the Realm

Tales From The Veil

with Corinne O'Flynn

The Portal Keepers

The Gimcrackers

Djinn Everlasting

Three Wishes

Forgotten Wishes

Hidden Wishes

Sisters of the Curse

Thea's Tale

One Night at the Ball

Casimir's Journey

Do you like being in the loop? Sign up for Lisa's newsletter! Shenanigans, book recs, and the latest news abound!

Want to see more of Lisa's books?

Visit www.Lisamanifold.com